# DOCTOR WHO
# AND THE
# GIANT ROBOT

*Also available in the Target series:*

# DOCTOR WHO
# AND THE
# GIANT ROBOT

Based on the BBC television serial *Doctor Who and the Robot* by Terrance Dicks by arrangement with the British Broadcasting Corporation.

## TERRANCE DICKS

To Dominic

Terrance Dicks

**TARGET**

A TARGET BOOK
published by
the Paperback Division of
W. H. ALLEN & Co. Ltd

A Target Book
Published in 1975
by the Paperback Division of W. H. Allen & Co. Ltd
A Howard & Wyndham Company
44 Hill Street, London W1X 8LB

Second impression 1979
Third impression 1980
Fourth impression 1981

Printed in Great Britain by
The Anchor Press Ltd,
Tiptree, Essex

ISBN 0 426 11279 2

# I

# Killer in the Night

It moved through the darkness, swift and silent despite its enormous bulk. Sensors fed a constant flow of information to the controlling brain: terrain underfoot uneven . . . irregular consistency . . . adjust balance mechanisms to compensate. Vegetable and organic matter impeding progress . . . resistance negligible . . . ignore. Objective in sight . . . one human guard armed with primitive weapon . . . prepare to neutralise . . .

The notice over the massively barred gate read,

### MINISTRY OF DEFENCE WEAPONRY RESEARCH CENTRE NO ADMITTANCE WITHOUT PASS

The sentry was bored and tired. How come *he* always got the night duty? Ruddy sergeant had it in for him, that's why. He sneaked a look at his watch. Another hour till the guard changed. Another hour stuck out here in the cold, windy darkness guarding a gate so strong that a tank couldn't get through it. So why guard it? He marched up and down glumly. Suddenly, he stopped. Something was moving, out there in the darkness. He strained his eyes. The area round the gate was brightly lit by an overhead lamp, but this only made the surrounding darkness all the blacker. But there *was* something . . .

Something huge, metallic . . . He raised his rifle, about to call out a challenge, when *it* stepped out of the darkness, and fear dried the words in his throat.

He stood frozen to the spot, unable to believe his eyes. The thing closed the distance between them in two swift strides. The sentry sucked in air to scream an alarm, but he was too late. A metal hand shot out and snapped his neck.

It caught the sentry as he fell and laid the body almost tenderly to one side. Then it moved forward to the gate. Having studied it for a moment, it reached out, and snapped the cable of the alarm system. Blue sparks flickered for a moment around the pincer-like fingers. It broke the heavy steel chains, smashed the lock from the gate, and pushed it open.

Gravel crunched beneath its feet as it moved up the drive towards the front door. It paused for a moment as the sensors detected movement. Some form of animal life was approaching . . .

An enormous black Doberman raced across the grounds, growling low in its throat. It was a particularly large and savage specimen of one of the fiercest breeds of guard dog in existence, and would have tackled anything from an armed man to a mountain lion without a second's hesitation. Yet, as it came up to its quarry it skidded to a halt, claws raking the gravel, scrabbling desperately to check its run. The dog backed away whimpering, then turned and fled in panic. The giant metal intruder smashed open the front door with a single massive blow and entered the building.

It moved along the corridors, infra-red vision taking it unerringly through the darkness. Soon it stood in an empty office, with a huge steel safe in the corner. The safe was the latest Government Security Model, guaranteed to resist thermic lances and high explosives. Metal

8

hands ripped the door from its hinges and reached inside. The shelves of the safe were stacked with buff-coloured folders, all bearing a red TOP SECRET stamp. Skilfully it sorted through the pile, extracted just one folder, and left the office. It moved out of the building, down the path, past the shattered gate and the dead sentry, and disappeared into the darkness.

The whole operation had taken place in a little under three minutes.

*　　*　　*　　*　　*

Brigadier Alastair Lethbridge-Stewart, head of the British Section of the United Nations Intelligence Taskforce (UNIT for short), stood in the empty laboratory and stared at a particular spot on the floor. On that spot he had seen something absolutely unbelievable happen. Now, several days later, he was reliving the scene, trying to convince himself that he could trust his own eyes.

It was after the peculiar business down at the meditation centre.* Yates had called in that journalist girl, Sarah Jane Smith, and she of course had involved the Doctor. The Brigadier still wasn't sure what had really happened. It seemed to be mixed up with a blue crystal from an alien planet, and some giant spiders who wanted the thing back. The Doctor had managed to clear things up, but he'd gone missing himself in the process. Just as they'd given him up for lost he'd reappeared again, but in a really shocking state, looking as if he was about to die on them.

And then . . . (The Brigadier frowned ferociously—he'd *seen* this last bit himself, and *still* didn't believe it) a little chap called Cho-Je, one of the monks from the Meditation Centre, had turned up, claiming to be a Time

* Told in DOCTOR WHO AND THE PLANET OF THE SPIDERS

Lord like the Doctor himself. Floating in mid air as cool as you please, he'd told them that the Doctor's old body was worn out by his exertions, and he'd have to trade it in for a new one . . .

The Brigadier had already adjusted to one change of appearance by the Doctor. It had taken him a long time to accept that the dark-haired, rather comical little chap who'd helped him against the Yeti and the Cybermen, and the tall white-haired man who'd turned up just in time to join the struggle against the Autons, were one and the same. Now he'd had to face another change. And *this* one had taken place under his very nose.

The Brigadier twitched that nose, and stared even harder at the piece of floor. In his mind's eye he could see the Doctor writhing and twisting in agony. He could see those familiar features begin to blur and change . . .

Suddenly it had been all over. A new man with a new face was lying on the laboratory floor. Like, and yet unlike. Still tall and thin, still with the same rather beaky nose. But a younger man, the face far less lined, a tangle of curly brown hair replacing the flowing white locks.

With Sarah Jane Smith kneeling beside him, the new Doctor had struggled to sit up. He was muttering something confused about 'Sontarans', and 'perverting the course of human history'. Benton had come in. Fixing him with an unnerving stare, the new Doctor had said distinctly, 'The Brontosaurus is large, placid and stupid,' and promptly collapsed. They'd rushed him off to the sick bay, and there he'd been ever since, lying in a kind of death-like coma. Young Dr. Sullivan, the new Medical Officer, was desperately worried about him. And so indeed was the Brigadier . . .

The opening of the laboratory door interrupted the Brigadier's musings. He turned and saw Sarah Jane Smith. Although she wasn't a member of UNIT, Sarah's friendship with the Doctor made her a kind of unofficial agent. The Brigadier harrumphed, somewhat embarrassed to be caught mooning about the empty laboratory. Gruffly he answered Sarah's unspoken question. 'Sorry, Miss Smith. No change. No change at all.'

Sarah sighed. For a moment there was an awkward silence. To break it the Brigadier said, 'Expect you're wondering what I'm doing here. Between you and me, I had a fit of absent-mindedness.' He tapped the Top Secret file tucked under his arm. 'Very unusual case here. Lots of baffling features. Soon as I read the reports I picked up the file and ...'

Sarah smiled understandingly. 'Came here to talk to the Doctor about it?'

The Brigadier nodded. 'Silly really. Poor old boy's in no state to talk about anything.'

'He'll be all right,' said Sarah. 'You remember Cho-Je said the change would shake him up a bit. He's bound to wake up soon.'

'Yes, of course,' said the Brigadier hastily. 'Only a matter of time.' Both spoke with a confidence they didn't feel. Both had heard ghastly stories about people who'd stayed in comas for years and years ...

A living death, thought Sarah, and shuddered. Just to change the subject, she asked, 'This case of yours, what was it all about?'

'Some plans were stolen from a Ministry of Defence Establishment.'

'Plans for what?'

'Something called a Disintegrator Gun. Miss Smith, this is all very top secret.'

Sarah couldn't resist teasing him. 'Then why did you tell me about it?'

'Well, because . . . because . . .' The Brigadier spluttered, at a loss for words. 'Because there's no one else here I *can* tell, I suppose.' He gestured eloquently round the empty laboratory. 'He used to drive me mad, you know, but I got used to having him about.' Sarah nodded sympathetically, realising how much the Brigadier must be missing his old friend. She changed the subject once again.

'As a matter of fact, I didn't *only* come to enquire about the Doctor. I wanted to ask a favour.' The Brigadier looked non-committal. Sarah gave him her most winning smile, and went on, 'You know that place they call the Thinktank? Frontiers-of-science research centre, all the latest in everything scientific under one roof?'

The Brigadier nodded. He knew the Thinktank only too well. It was one of his recurring problems. A few years ago, the Government had realised that a number of different firms, and different Government departments too, were all working separately in much the same fields. Obviously it was only sensible to end such wasteful duplication, pool the effort, and share the results. To do this, the Thinktank had been created. Top research scientists from both public and private establishments now all worked together under the same roof. Both Government and Industry shared the expenses and the benefits of their work. The Thinktank was a typically British institution: it was ramshackle and illogical, but it worked. But it was something of a nightmare from the security point of view. Quite a bit of top-secret research went on there, which meant that it occasionally came into the Brigadier's area of interest. The problem was that the Thinktank people had developed strong internal loyalties, and were fiercely resentful of what they called 'interference'. Since the place was only partly under Government control, the Brigadier had to deal with them tactfully. The Thinktank had good contacts and powerful friends in high places, and didn't scruple to call on them if it felt its precious independence was under attack.

All this ran through the Brigadier's head in a matter of seconds. He looked at Sarah warily. 'Yes, Miss Smith, I know the Thinktank. As a matter of fact, they developed these plans that have been stolen. What about the place?'

'Well, now and again, exceptionally favoured journalists are allowed to visit it,' said Sarah hopefully.

The Brigadier stared blankly at her for a moment, and then smiled. 'You want me to get you a visitor's pass?'

'Please. You see, I'm very keen to get away from all this woman's angle stuff, and if I could come up with a really good *scientific* story . . .'

'I think we can arrange that for you, Miss Smith. Come to my office and I'll fix you up with a pass.'

Sarah followed him out of the laboratory. 'Could I *see* the Doctor before I go?'

'Yes, of course. You'll find it a bit depressing though. Poor old chap just lies there . . .'


On the other side of the building, in the UNIT sick bay, the Doctor lay flat on his back on the bed, nose and toes pointing at the ceiling. Suddenly his eyes snapped wide open. He looked at the ceiling. He looked round the bare hospital-like room. He took a deep breath, feeling air flooding deep into his lungs. He stretched and wriggled, aware of the steady double beat of his hearts, the strength and vigour in his muscles. A huge delighted grin spread over his face, and he sprang out of bed like a jack-in-the-box. For a moment he stood there in his striped pyjamas, as if uncertain what to do next. There was a locker beside the bed. He opened it and looked inside. Clothes. A velvet smoking jacket, check trousers, a frilly shirt. The Doctor fingered the elegant garments for a moment and frowned. They looked as if they'd fit all right, but he didn't *like* them. Far too fancy. What sort of a chap would go around dressed up like that? Still, it didn't matter. He had lots more clothes in . . . in . . . in the TARDIS! The Doctor beamed. Of course, that's where he should be, off in the TARDIS, not hanging about round here! He grabbed the jacket, slung it carelessly round his shoulders, picked up a pair of elastic-sided boots from the bottom of the locker, and strode briskly out of the room.

He found himself in a long featureless corridor, the walls painted a depressing olive green. For a moment the Doctor panicked. He realised he had no idea where to go. Then a picture of the TARDIS sitting in the corner of the laboratory popped into his head. At the same time the route to it began to unfold clearly in his mind. Although the Doctor's memory was still a little cloudy, it was obviously prepared to tell him everything he needed to know. Much reassured, the Doctor set off on his way.

The Brigadier finished filling out a complicated-looking form, signed it, walloped it with a number of Government stamps, and handed it over to Sarah. 'There you are. Show them that at the main gate, and they'll endorse it for the length of your visit. Now let's take a look at the Doctor. Young Sullivan should be with him by now.'

As she followed the Brigadier towards the sick bay, Sarah asked, 'Are you sure he's the right man to look after the Doctor?'

'Dr. Sullivan? First-class chap. Very fine doctor, too. What's the matter with him?'

For a moment Sarah didn't reply. She'd met Dr. Sullivan, formerly Lieutenant Sullivan of the Royal Navy, on a previous visit. He was a big, breezy young man with a square jaw, blue eyes, fair curly hair and a hearty manner. Sarah thought he looked rather like the hero of a *Boy's Own Paper* adventure yarn. He immediately made you think of Biggles or Bulldog Drummond. She struggled to express her doubts without upsetting the Brigadier. 'Isn't he a bit—old-fashioned?'

The Brigadier frowned down at her. 'Nothing wrong with that, Miss Smith. You may not have noticed, but I'm a little old-fashioned myself!'

Sarah chuckled. She always appreciated the Brigadier's rare, dead-pan jokes. 'Never! You're a swinger, Brigadier.' Then she returned to the attack. 'All the same —for a complicated case like the Doctor's . . .'

'Miss Smith, do you think there's a specialist in England, in the world, who's capable of understanding what's happened to the Doctor?'

Silently Sarah shook her head. The Brigadier was of course right. They didn't teach bodily regeneration in the medical schools. Not on this planet, anyway.


Around the corner, the Doctor heard their approach. Instinctively he ducked into a storeroom, and waited until the sounds died away. Then he emerged and, boots still in hand, tiptoed silently along in his bare feet. A few minutes later, he was cautiously opening the laboratory door. He peered in, saw the place was empty, and slipped inside, closing the door behind him. For a moment he paused, as if not quite sure why he was there. He saw the familiar square, blue shape in the corner. Of course. The TARDIS! He crossed the room and tried to open the TARDIS door. It was locked. The Doctor frowned.

'Key,' he said to himself rapidly. 'Key, key, key!' He stood for a moment, running his fingers through his tangled mop of curly hair. Then he smiled, nodded, and tipped up one of the boots he was carrying. The TARDIS key dropped into his palm. 'Yes, of course. Obvious place.'

As he put the key in the lock, the laboratory door opened. The Doctor whirled round. Harry Sullivan, white-coated, stethoscope round his neck, full of professional cheerfulness, stood in the doorway, wagging a reproving finger.

'I thought as much. Come on, Doctor, you're supposed to be in bed.'

The Doctor looked at him blankly. 'Am I? Why?'

Harry's voice was infuriatingly soothing. 'Because you're not fit yet.'

'Fit?' said the Doctor indignantly. 'Fit? Of course I'm fit.' He began running on the spot with great rapidity. Then he touched his toes ten times, did ten push-ups, sprang to his feet and marched up to Harry with a triumphant grin. 'You see? All systems go!' Before Harry could speak, the Doctor reached for his stethoscope. Deftly he popped the earpieces into Harry's ears, and applied the other end to his own chest. Bemused, Harry heard a steady thump, thump, thump—the beat of a strong and healthy heart. The Doctor moved the stethoscope to the right side of his own chest. Harry heard *another* thump, thump, thump, 'I say,' he said, 'I don't think that can be right.'

'Both a bit fast, I expect,' said the Doctor thoughtfully. 'Still, must be patient. A new body's like a new house. Bound to take a while to settle in.'

Handing back the stethoscope, the Doctor wandered across to a wall mirror. He examined his own face critically, as though it was that of a stranger—as indeed it was in a way. 'As for the face—well, you have to take the rough with the smooth. Mind you, I think the nose is definitely an improvement. But the ears now—frankly I'm not too sure about the ears.' The Doctor gave the ears an experimental tug, seemed to accept that they were fixed, and turned back to Harry. 'Tell me frankly—what do *you* think about the ears?'

Harry had been watching the Doctor with a mixture of amazement and professional interest. 'Hyper-active, poor chap,' he was thinking. 'Body's been at a standstill, now it's suddenly gone into top gear. He'll crack up if I don't get him sedated.'

The sudden question about the ears threw him completely. 'Well, I . . . er . . . I don't really know . . .'

'Of course you don't,' said the Doctor briskly. 'You're a busy man. You don't want to stand here burbling about my ears.' He nudged Harry's ribs with a bony elbow. 'I mean—it's neither *'ere* nor there, is it?' Smiling delightedly at his own little joke, the Doctor grabbed Harry's right hand and shook it vigorously.

'Well, thank you for a most enjoyable little chat. Now I'm afraid I must be on my way.'

Harry, who had been standing there wide-eyed and open-mouthed, suddenly came to life. He jumped in front of the Doctor, barring the way to the TARDIS. 'I'm sorry, Doctor, but there's no question of you going anywhere—except back to the sick bay. You're going to go back to bed, and you're going to stay there till *I* say you can get up.'

Harry Sullivan was a powerful young man in top physical condition. In his service days he had often boxed for the Navy. He advanced determinedly on the Doctor, quite prepared to use force if he had to. After all, it was for the patient's own good.

\*     \*     \*     \*     \*

Sarah and the Brigadier gazed in astonishment at the empty room, and the empty bed. The Brigadier's mind flashed back several years. Once before, the Doctor had recovered with amazing speed from a death-like coma, and had fled from a hospital bed with one thought in his mind. 'Come on,' he said. 'He'll be making for the TARDIS.'

After a breathless sprint through the corridors of UNIT, Sarah and the Brigadier crashed into the laboratory. For a moment, it seemed the Brigadier was wrong. The laboratory was silent, the TARDIS still in its usual corner. They heard a muffled thumping from a cupboard. The Brigadier opened it and Harry Sullivan fell out. The Brigadier fielded him neatly, and set him back on his feet.

Sullivan was spluttering with indignation. 'Picked me up,' he said with a sort of astonished rage. 'Picked me up and chucked me in the cupboard like—like a ruddy old coat!'

'Where *is* he?' asked Sarah. A familiar groaning sound from the corner answered the question for her. The TARDIS was beginning to shudder and vibrate.

'Too late!' said the Brigadier. 'He's off again!'

## 2

## Something *More* than Human

Sarah couldn't bear the thought of losing the Doctor so soon. She remembered Cho-Je's words. If the Doctor *was* still weak and irrational it would be sheer madness to let him go rushing off. She ran to the TARDIS and started hammering on the door. 'Doctor, please wait! Don't go! Please, you've got to listen!'

Inside the TARDIS, the Doctor stood at the control console, his hands flickering over the controls. He paused, his finger poised over the switch that would send the TARDIS spinning off into the depths of the Time Vortex. Faintly, he heard the hammering on the door, and the sound of Sarah's voice. He reached for the switch, then withdrew his hand. There was something about that voice, some note of anguish or appeal that was difficult to ignore. He put the TARDIS on shut-down, and pressed the control which opened the door.

Sarah was overjoyed when the take-off sound died away and the TARDIS stopped vibrating. Suddenly the door opened, and a head popped out. Sarah stepped back, a little alarmed. The Doctor had certainly come out of his coma—right out. The unfamiliar face was bright and alert, the blue eyes sparkling. Even the curly hair seemed to be standing on end with sheer energy!

The Doctor surveyed his audience of three and said briskly, 'Come to see me off, eh? Well, it's very kind of you, but I hate farewells. I'll just slip quietly away, shall I? Goodbye!'

The head withdrew and the TARDIS door started to close. Sarah called, 'Doctor—you can't go!'

The head emerged again. 'Can't I? Why not?' The Doctor looked intently at Sarah, obviously waiting for an answer.

'Why not, indeed?' thought Sarah. If the Doctor was really determined to go, how could they stop him? She racked her brains for a convincing reply. 'Well, because . . . er . . . because the Brigadier needs you.' She threw Lethbridge-Stewart a frantic glance, mutely begging him to back her up.

The Brigadier did his best. 'What? Oh yes, yes, of course. Depending on you!'

The Doctor's keen eyes turned to the Brigadier. 'Are you? What for?'

The Brigadier had no idea how to answer this question, and gave Sarah a look of anguished enquiry.

Sarah's mind shot back to their earlier conversation. If they could only persuade the Doctor that he was staying for *their* sake rather than his own ... 'There's been this robbery,' she said. 'It's all very important and hush-hush. Isn't that right, Brigadier?'

The Brigadier realised what Sarah was up to. 'Quite right,' he confirmed. 'Very serious business. Relying on your help, Doctor.'

The Doctor looked thoughtful. Sarah pressed home her advantage. 'I mean you *are* still UNIT's Scientific Adviser. You can't go off and leave them in the lurch just at the time when they...'

Her voice tailed off as she realised that the Doctor had stopped listening. He came out of the TARDIS and walked up to the Brigadier, peering intently into his face. The Brigadier backed away a little nervously. 'Wait a moment, old chap,' said the Doctor, 'I know you, don't I?'

'Well of course you do,' snapped the Brigadier.

The Doctor scratched his chin. 'Now don't tell me ... Military man, am I right? Hannibal? No, wrong period. Alexander the Great? Still wrong. Got it! Lethbridge-Stewart! Brigadier Alastair Lethbridge-Stewart!'

Pleased that his erratic memory had come up with another correct item of information, the Doctor shook the Brigadier warmly by the hand. Then he turned to Sarah. 'And Sarah Jane Smith! Well, well, well, this is quite a reunion!' He stretched out his other arm and drew Sarah to him in a friendly bear-hug.

Sarah was overjoyed. 'Doctor, you *know* us!'

'Well of course I do,' said the Doctor, as if the matter had never been in doubt.

Harry Sullivan, feeling rather out of things, looked on as the three old friends exchanged delighted greetings. Suddenly the Doctor said, 'Well, this is all very pleasant, but we're not here to socialise. We've got a job to do.'

Sarah and the Brigadier exchanged worried glances.

'Well,' said the Doctor impatiently, 'what's all this about a robbery?'

*     *     *     *     *

This time the notice read 'MINISTRY OF DEFENCE STORAGE WAREHOUSE. NO ADMITTANCE.' The concrete posts of the heavy wire fence held other notices, each surmounted with a skull and crossbones. 'WARNING! ELECTRIFIED FENCE. DO NOT TOUCH. DANGER OF DEATH.' The fence ran across the edge of a lonely moor, covered with drifting patches of mist.

Two huge, metallic hands reached out and snapped the thick wires like strands of cotton. Blue sparks crackled round metal fingers. A huge, gleaming shape moved through the gap and set off towards a long, low building.

The warehouse was really a converted concrete bunker. It had been an ammunition dump before the Ministry had taken it over for storage. In the warehouse, the alarm bell had been triggered off by the cutting of the wire fence. As soon as the guard on duty, a tough, competent ex-warrant officer, heard the alarm ringing he followed standing orders and closed the security door. He waited calmly, knowing that the top-secret equipment it was his duty to protect would be safe behind the massive concrete walls and the heavy door of reinforced steel. Someone would let him know when the emergency was over. Until then he'd sit tight, as ordered.

Suddenly, he heard a massive thump, thump, thump outside the door. Like the sound of giant footsteps. To his amazement he watched as the massive steel security doors slowly buckled inwards. With a screech of ripped metal, they were flung open. Before he had time to take in the full horror of the thing looming in the doorway, its metal hands reached out for him . . . When the guard was dead, it lowered him almost tenderly to the floor. It disliked harming a living creature, but it knew that certain things were necessary. Smoothly it swung round to face the shelves. Row upon row of electronic parts were stored in labelled boxes. It began scanning the shelves quickly, taking only the equipment it needed. It filled an empty crate with its selection, left the bunker and disappeared into the mist.

\*     \*     \*     \*     \*

Harry Sullivan sat perched on a laboratory stool, elbows on knees, chin in hands, fixing the TARDIS with an unblinking stare. He *knew* it couldn't really vanish into thin air as the others had told him. But he was taking no chances. Moreover, he had been ordered not to let the Doctor out of his sight, and keeping an eye on the TARDIS was the best he could do at the moment.

The Brigadier rushed in, a message form in his hands and an expression of anger on his face. Harry slid off the stool and came to attention. The Brigadier waved him back to his seat, and Harry obeyed, thinking he'd never get used to UNIT's lack of formality.

The Brigadier glanced rapidly round the room. 'Where is he?'

'In there, sir.' Harry nodded towards the TARDIS.

22

The Brigadier exploded. 'Why on earth didn't you stop him?'

Harry glanced at the cupboard. 'I tried that once before, sir. Anyway, he said . . .'

The TARDIS door opened to reveal the Doctor. He was wearing furry trousers, a bearskin jacket and a Viking helmet.

The Brigadier said, 'Doctor, there's been another . . .' His voice tailed off as he took in the full splendour of the Doctor's appearance, then he gulped helplessly.

The Doctor looked at him with concern. 'Something the matter, old chap?'

'You've—changed,' said the Brigadier, hoarsely.

The Doctor looked alarmed. 'Not again, surely!' He dashed across the room and peered in the mirror. 'No, no, you're mistaken. The regeneration's quite stable.'

The Brigadier controlled himself. 'I was referring to your clothes, Doctor, not your face.'

The Doctor studied the Brigadier's anguished expression. 'You don't like them?'

The Brigadier cleared his throat. 'Well, it's not that, Doctor, but UNIT *is* supposed to be an undercover organisation.'

'Ah,' said the Doctor shrewdly, 'you think I might attract undue attention?'

The Brigadier's moustache twitched. 'It's just possible that you might,' he answered gravely.

'A good point,' said the Doctor. 'One moment, please.'

He disappeared inside the TARDIS and a moment later reappeared in a Roman toga, complete with laurel wreath. The Brigadier didn't trust himself to speak. He began turning an alarming shade of purple.

'No?' asked the Doctor. He looked at the Brigadier, then at Harry. 'No!' he answered himself, and popped back into the TARDIS.

In an amazingly short time he reappeared in another outfit. This time he wore wide corduroy trousers, a sort of tweed hacking-jacket with a vaguely Edwardian look, and a loose flannel shirt. A wide-brimmed floppy black hat and an immensely long scarf completed the ensemble. Before the Brigadier could speak, Harry said quickly, 'That's *much* better, Doctor.' He shot a warning glance at the Brigadier. Eccentric as the Doctor's outfit was, it did at least bear a passing resemblance to present-day dress. Another try might produce something far worse— a suit of chain-mail, for instance.

'You're sure?' asked the Doctor amiably. 'I'll try again if you like. Lots more stuff in there, you know.'

The Brigadier shuddered, reaching the same conclusion as Harry. 'That'll do very well, Doctor. Now if we've settled the matter of your wardrobe, I came to tell you there's been another . . .'

The Doctor was already on his way out of the room. 'Come along, Lethbridge-Stewart. Time we were off.'

'Off where?' spluttered the Brigadier, dashing after him. Harry followed them into the corridor.

'We must of course visit the scene of the crime.'

'Which one?' said the Brigadier, struggling to catch up with him. 'Thing is, there's been a second robbery.'

The Doctor was disappearing down the corridor, his long scarf flowing out behind him. His voice floated over his shoulder. 'Tell me on the way, Brigadier, tell me on the way. You really must cultivate a sense of urgency.' Convinced by now that he had left the Navy for something very like a lunatic asylum, Harry Sullivan ran after them.

Some hours later, after a long cold drive, all three were sitting in the Brigadier's Land-Rover. They had parked close by the gap in the electric fence. Swirls of mist were still drifting over the moor. The Brigadier gestured towards the ragged fence. 'Millions of volts running through that blessed thing, yet for all the good . . .' He became aware that the Doctor seemed to have vanished, and said enquiringly, 'Doctor? Where are you?'

Harry tapped him respectfully on the shoulder, and pointed downwards. The Doctor had jumped out of the Land-Rover and was sitting cross-legged on the damp grass, staring raptly at something on the palm of his hand. Harry shook his head sadly. He wasn't surprised. Poor chap should still be in bed. The excitement had obviously been too much for him.

The Brigadier jumped from behind the wheel and stood beside the Doctor.

'Doctor, will you please pay attention !'

'Oh, but I am, I assure you. Look !' Uncoiling his long legs, the Doctor rose to his feet and held out his hand. The Brigadier bent over to look. In his palm the Doctor held a daisy. It had been squashed completely flat, like a pressed flower in a book.

The Brigadier snorted. 'I have every respect for your concern for the ecology, Doctor, but at a time like this, the importance of one squashed daisy . . .'

'Not just *squashed*,' interrupted the Doctor mildly, '*flattened*. Almost pulverised. Now, how did it get like that ?'

Harry climbed out of the Land-Rover and joined them. 'I assume it was stepped on.'

'Exactly. And according to my estimate of the resistance of vegetable fibre to pressure, it was stepped on by something that weighed a quarter of a ton.' Striding through the gap in the wire, the Doctor disappeared into the mist.

Harry and the Brigadier followed him across the compound and up to the shattered metal door of the bunker. The Doctor paused to examine the broken edges of the metal. 'Not cut, or blown open,' he said thoughtfully. *'Torn!'*

He went inside the bunker and stood gazing at the long rows of shelves.

The Brigadier sorted through the file of reports he was carrying. 'Funny thing is they left a lot of extremely valuable and top-secret stuff behind. Here's a list of everything that was actually taken.'

The Doctor scanned the list rapidly. 'Very selective thief. Miniaturised atomic power pack, and all the equipment you'd need for the control circuitry of one compact, powerful, technological device. A Disintegrator Gun, for instance.' He handed the list back and strode towards the door. 'Might as well get back, Brigadier. There's nothing more to be learned here.'

As they drove towards UNIT H.Q. the Brigadier said, 'So what are we looking for, Doctor?'

The Doctor was sprawled in the back seat, hat over his eyes and apparently asleep, but his answer came immediately. 'Something intelligent that takes only what it needs, and leaves the rest. Something that kills a man as casually as it crushes a daisy.'

Harry shivered. 'What sort of something? Is it human?'

The Doctor shook his head. 'I doubt it. Something more than human, perhaps.'

The Brigadier said, 'Well, whatever it is, how do we find it?'

'We could try locking the *next* stable door in good time.'

'Never mind the riddles, Doctor . . .'

The Doctor continued calmly, '*It*—whatever *It* may be—has stolen the plans for the Disintegrator Gun, the equipment necessary for control circuitry, and the atomic power to make it work. I therefore assume it intends to build the gun. Now if I'm right, and I invariably am, what is the third vital ingredient?' the Doctor folded his arms and sat back. Harry was baffled, but the Brigadier's response was immediate.

'Good grief—the focussing generator!'

'Exactly!' The Doctor smiled benignly, like a teacher who sees a dimmish pupil grasp a simple theorem.

The Brigadier snatched the radio-mike from the dashboard. 'Greyhound Leader to Trap One. Red Priority.'

After a moment the voice of the UNIT radio operator at H.Q. crackled back. 'Trap One. We read you, Greyhound Leader.'

'Get me Sergeant Benton.'

After a moment, another voice came through. 'Benton here, sir.'

The Brigadier snapped, 'That factory in Essex, Benton. Place where they make the focussing generators. Know it?'

'I know it, sir.'

'I want a full security seal. Liaise with the Regulars and get me every available man. Air Cover as well! I'll rendezvous with you there in one hour. By then I want that place sealed tighter than Fort Knox. Greyhound out.'

As the Brigadier slammed back the radio mike, the Land-Rover came to a crossroads. Harry and the Doctor clutched the sides for support as the Brigadier spun the wheel, sending them roaring down the misty road towards Essex.

# 3

# Trouble at Thinktank

Hilda Winters stood at the office window and looked out. The rolling grounds of the big, old country house stretched far away into the distance. White-coated technicians hurried along the gravel paths that linked the various outbuildings. Not for the first time, she thought how lucky she was to be working here in the country, rather than in some featureless London office block.

The Thinktank had started life as a manor house, built by a wealthy merchant in the spacious days of the nineteenth century. Now, in the twentieth, it was far too expensive for any private owner to keep up. Like many other big houses, it had been taken over by the Government. Its size and relative isolation made it an ideal choice for the newly-founded Thinktank. Now the sprawling wings of the main building, and the many stables, barns, outhouses, potting sheds, and greenhouses, had all been converted into ultra-modern laboratories. Mercifully, the conversion had been carried out unobtrusively, and, except for the addition of a guarded perimeter fence, the outside of the fine old building was unchanged. The Director's office, once the Squire's study, was also very much the same, except for the addition of a few filing cabinets.

Miss Winters heard a nervous cough behind her, and turned away from the window. Jellicoe, the Thinktank Public Relations Officer, was hovering in the doorway. He was a nervous, fussy man in his late thirties, who combed his thinning fair hair carefully across a spreading bald patch, and made the mistake of dressing in clothes far too elaborately trendy for his age. His eyes were a watery blue, his mouth thin and cruel.

Miss Winters sighed. Jellicoe was hard-working and willing, but somehow he always seemed to get on her nerves.

'That journalist girl's arrived,' he said. 'The one with the UNIT pass—they telephoned about her.'

Miss Winters said nothing. She never wasted words.

Jellicoe floundered on. 'It's something of a nuisance—at the present moment in time. One hopes it's no more than coincidence.'

'If UNIT intended to investigate us, they could find better agents than a freelance female journalist.'

'I suppose so, I suppose so. Still, you can't deny it's worrying. When we've reached such a crucial stage . . .'

Miss Winters' voice was crisp. 'Visiting journalists are *your* responsibility. But if it will make you any happier, I'll accompany you on the tour.'

'Would you?' said Jellicoe eagerly. 'She's at Reception now.'

Waiting in the Reception area, Sarah thought that the Brigadier had no need to worry about Thinktank security. It seemed to be red hot. Her pass had been examined very thoroughly by a tough-looking security guard, phone calls had been made, and finally the pass had been handed back marked VALID ONE DAY ONLY.

Another guard had taken her into Reception, delivering a stern warning that she must go nowhere without an official guide. She was told the Director would be with her shortly—in tones that suggested she was unworthy of such an honour. All in all, Sarah's reception at the Thinktank had put her in a rather hostile mood, though she found it hard to pin down any specific reason. Sternly she told herself that she was lucky to be here at all, and that no doubt all these people were just doing their job.

Two figures came down the wide staircase towards her: a trendy, over-dressed man in his thirties and an attractive dark-haired woman of about the same age, looking cool and elegant in a formal business costume. 'One of your top Civil Service secretaries, no doubt,' thought Sarah. She rose to her feet as the two approached and held out her hand to the man. 'It's very kind of you to allow this visit, Director,' she said, determined to make a good impression from the start. She knew at once that she had made a mistake. The man simply shuffled and looked embarrassed. The woman spoke with quiet amusement.

'I didn't expect male chauvinism from you, Miss Smith.'

Confused, Sarah said, 'I'm sorry?'

'I'm Hilda Winters, the Director. This is Mr. Jellicoe, our Public Relations Officer.'

Sarah was furious, with them and with herself. It had been foolish of her to assume that the man was inevitably the Director. But she felt that the two of them had expected the mistake, and were using it to put her in her place. Smiling to conceal her annoyance, she said sweetly, 'Do forgive me—such a stupid mistake.'

'Not at all,' said Miss Winters with equal sweetness. 'Shall we begin the tour?'

An hour later, Sarah was tired, footsore and in a worse temper than ever. Jellicoe and Miss Winters had marched her briskly in and out of an endless succession of laboratories, and shown her an equal number of boring and incomprehensible experiments concerned with such worthy but undramatic subjects as new fuels, building materials and foodstuffs. Her eyes ached from peering at dials, charts and computers. They'd soon discovered her lack of formal scientific training, and instead of simplifying their explanations, had taken every opportunity to bombard her with scientific data. The worse thing of all was the fact that it had all been a complete waste of time. For all she had learned from her visit, she might just as well have sat at home reading one of Jellicoe's glossy Public Relations handouts. Despite her attempts to draw them out, both her guides had been blandly unco-operative. She had nothing that any editor would recognise as a 'story'.

The last stop on the tour had been a biology laboratory in a converted greenhouse at the far end of the extensive grounds, where they were developing a new high-yield wheat. As she trailed wearily back towards the main gate, her guides continued to lecture her in their blandly superior manner.

'Yes, we do mostly 'frontiers-of-science' type research here,' said Jellicoe. 'Not easy for the layman—or lay-woman—to understand.'

Smoothly Miss Winters took over. 'Mind you, we only do the preliminary theoretical work here. As soon as our work reaches the practical stage, we have to hand it over to someone with more resources and a bigger budget—usually the Government.'

Almost without thinking, Sarah said, 'Like the new Disintegrator Gun? You pioneered the research on that, didn't you?'

She saw a look of surprise, almost of alarm, pass between them. 'As a matter of fact we did,' said Miss Winters slowly. 'Though I'm not at all sure you should know that.'

Sarah felt she'd somehow gained the initiative. 'Oh I have my sources,' she said airily. She had a sudden impulse to increase their discomfiture. They were passing the open door of a long low building, apparently disused. 'What's in here?' asked Sarah brightly. Before anyone could stop her, she popped inside.

She found herself in a spotlessly clean, empty concrete room. A long central work-bench held clamps, lathes, vices, and other metal-working equipment. Facing her in the opposite wall was a pair of heavy metal doors. The windowless room was lit by overhead fluorescent lighting which gleamed coldly off the metal surfaces. The whole place reminded her more of a garage workshop than a laboratory. Everything had a solid, practical air. Jellicoe and Miss Winters had followed her in, and were now hovering agitatedly round her, trying to edge her towards the door. 'What goes on here then?' she asked, refusing to be budged.

'Nothing goes on here,' said Miss Winters coldly. 'As you can see, this section is currently disused.'

'Weren't you telling me earlier that pressure on space was your greatest problem? I'm surprised you haven't found a use for a room like this.'

Jellicoe and Miss Winters exchanged glances. Sarah could almost feel the tension crackling between them. She wandered over to a board and looked at a faded notice. 'J. P. Kettlewell, Robotics Section,' she read out loud. Sarah wrinkled her forehead, remembering. 'Oh yes, he left you some time ago, didn't he? There was quite a fuss about it in the papers.'

'Indeed there was,' said Miss Winters, visibly controlling herself. 'If you remember, he turned against conventional science altogether.'

Jellicoe joined in with a shaky laugh. 'That's right. Spent his time researching into "alternative technology" —whatever that's supposed to mean.'

Sarah wandered towards the metal doors. 'What's through there?' Jellicoe slipped in front of her, barring her way. 'Storeroom,' he said rapidly. 'Professor Kettlewell left some valuable equipment there. We're responsible for it, until he deigns to come and collect it.'

Miss Winters indicated the door. 'We *must* be on our way, Miss Smith. Your little tour is over now. I imagine you have work to do—and I know I have.'

Sarah felt she'd better give way gracefully. 'Yes, of course—and thank you again for all your kindness. It's been most—' She broke off as one leg shot out from under her. Jellicoe jumped forward and grabbed her elbow, saving her from what would have been a nasty fall. 'Are you all right?'

Sarah gasped. 'Just about—thank you.'

'Dangerous business, wandering round places you don't know.' Sarah sensed the threat in his words.

Miss Winters took a firm grip on Sarah's other elbow. 'You're lucky you weren't badly hurt.' Flanking her like guards, Jellicoe and Miss Winters marched Sarah from the room.

As she drove away from Thinktank—after a series of mutually insincere thanks and farewells—Sarah knew that her journalistic instincts had been fully roused. There *was* a story after all, and somehow or other she'd stumbled on to it. Something to do with that empty Robotics Section—and Professor Kettlewell. It was true that Kettlewell *had* left the Thinktank in a huff quite some time ago, loudly broadcasting that all conventional science was dragging mankind down the road to ruin. But *why* hadn't they turned his workshop over to someone else? And *why* had there been a patch of fresh machine oil for her to slip on? Sarah told herself that, as evidence, it was all pretty flimsy.

But the waves of alarm that she had felt emanating from Winters and Jellicoe, and the tension and strain which had been in the air during her few minutes in Kettlewell's workshop, had convinced her that something shifty was going on.

She parked her car beside a roadside callbox and telephoned a friend in the reference department of one of the national papers. A few minutes later she was scribbling Kettlewell's address in her notebook. She got back in her car and checked her AA map. He lived on the outskirts of a little village, about thirty miles away. She looked at her watch. Quite a drive there and back, and then on to London. Still, a story was a story. And the thought of getting the better of that smug pair at Thinktank justified any amount of effort. Full of professional zeal, Sarah started the car.

\* \* \* \* \*

Harry Sullivan sat shivering in the passenger seat of the Brigadier's Land-Rover, and wished he'd stopped to grab an overcoat before their mad dash from UNIT. Beside him the Brigadier was studying a map, seemingly impervious to the evening chill. In the back seat, the Doctor sprawled dozing, his hat over his eyes.

They had parked in a patch of woodland just outside a small factory compound. It was late afternoon and darkness was gathering rapidly, blurring the outlines of buildings and trees. From the gloom all around them Harry could hear the sounds of stealthy movement: the tramp of booted feet, the clinking of metal on metal, and occasionally a muttered password. Helicopters on patrol droned steadily overhead. 'It seems an awful lot of fuss to protect one little electronics factory,' he said. 'Are you sure it's worth it?'

The Doctor's voice came from behind him. 'The Disintegrator Gun works by focussing and condensing a beam of energy in such a way that it strikes the target with colossal force. To do this it utilises a device known as a focussing generator. These devices are manufactured *only* in the factory you see before you. Correct, Brigadier?'

34

The Brigadier grunted and went on reading his map. Undeterred, the Doctor continued his lecture. 'Our unknown opponent has stolen the plans for the Disintegrator Gun, *and* the miniaturised atomic power unit with its control circuitry. To complete the assembly of the gun, one thing more is needed—a focussing generator! Which can only be obtained *here*. Hence the display of military might, with which the Brigadier hopes to render this impossible!'

The Brigadier looked up from his map. 'More than "hopes", Doctor. No one, *nothing*, could succeed in breaking into that factory.'

The Doctor yawned and stretched. 'I admire your confidence.'

'Armed guards have every inch of the perimeter under observation. There are helicopter patrols overhead.' Warming to his subject, the Brigadier tapped his mapcase with his swagger stick. 'Inside that factory is a vault. Not just a safe, Doctor, a vault, with a sentry outside the door. Inside the vault is a sealed metal casket, containing every blessed focussing generator in the place. Believe me, the place is *impregnable*.'

The Doctor scratched his nose thoughtfully. 'Never cared for words like "impregnable" myself. Too much like "unsinkable".'

Harry looked at him in amazement. 'What's the matter with "unsinkable"?'

'Reminds me of the *Titanic*. You know—glug, glug, glug!'

A large figure materialised silently from the gloom and saluted. The Brigadier looked up eagerly. 'Ah, Benton. All patrols posted?'

Sergeant Benton nodded. 'They're practically standing on each other's toes, sir!'

Triumphantly the Brigadier turned to the Doctor.

'You see? Not even a rat could get through that cordon. The place is protected from every side, *and* from above.'

The Doctor nodded. Then he sat up suddenly, as a new thought seemed to strike him.

'That still leaves one direction, doesn't it?'

'What do you mean?'

Silently the Doctor pointed a long finger—straight down at the ground.

The young sentry guarding the factory vault had been assured he was on to a cushy number. 'Look at it this way,' Sergeant Benton had advised. 'We're ringed out there three-deep. Anything that gets to you, son, has got to come through us first.' It had seemed to make sense at the time. But now, after half an hour of lonely guard duty, the sentry was beginning to feel nervous. According to all the rumours, they were expecting an attack from something pretty fearsome—and *he* was the one guarding what it was after.

Suddenly the sentry froze, listening. Sounds, muffled thumping sounds, were coming from inside the vault. He listened—silence. Then it started again. Or did it? Was it just his imagination? He thought of calling the guard sergeant. But suppose he *was* imagining it all? Maybe it would be wiser to check—he didn't want to make a fool of himself.

He unlocked the vault, and spun the heavy wheel that opened the door. Cautiously, he slipped inside. Everything seemed normal. The metal casket with its precious contents stood on the table—just as he'd last seen it. Then the muffled thumping started again. It grew louder, louder still. It was coming from beneath his feet! Unbelievingly, the sentry watched as the concrete floor of the vault was burst open from below. A jagged hole appeared—and through it a massive metal hand reached out towards him. Terrified, the sentry blazed away with his sub-machine gun . . .

# 4

## Robot!

The Doctor, Harry and the Brigadier heard the shots from the Land-Rover—followed by a high, choking scream. The Doctor jumped out and began running towards the factory, his long legs covering the ground at an astonishing rate. The Brigadier and Harry dashed after him.

Outside the vault, Benton and a group of soldiers were trying to batter down the door with a heavy metal work-bench.

'Door's been opened from the *outside*, sir,' panted Benton. 'Then jammed again from the *inside*. There's something in there all right. Something big. We heard it moving. Come on, lads, heave! You're like a lot of ruddy schoolgirls.' Propelled by the arms of six brawny soldiers, the heavy bench crashed against the vault door. Two more collisions, and the door gave way with a ripping of metal. Jammed all together, guns at the ready, the little group burst into the vault.

It was empty—except for the crumpled body of the sentry in one corner. In the centre of the floor yawned a huge, jagged hole. The metal casket had disappeared.

The Doctor peered thoughtfully in to the hole. 'There seems to be a very large rat about, Brigadier. Possibly we should obtain the services of a very large cat!'

Furiously the Brigadier turned to Sergeant Benton. 'Search the area. I want the other end of that tunnel found—immediately!

Half an hour later, the tunnel was discovered. No attempt had been made to conceal it. The ragged hole, about six feet in diameter, plunged straight in to the side of a little hill which overlooked the factory. Lights were rigged up, and a UNIT patrol swarmed over it with metal-detecting equipment—but they found nothing. 'Thing is, sir,' said Benton, 'it's not a proper tunnel at all. No props or anything. Just the earth shoved aside and left to cave in. Whoever went through it wouldn't be able to breath.'

The Doctor nodded, unsurprised. 'Whoever went through it didn't need to breathe.'

Benton led them to the far edge of the hole. 'And we found these, sir.' A line of footprints led towards the woods, too large and too widely spaced to have been made by anything human. 'They fade away in the woods. Ground's covered with leaves, won't take prints.'

The Doctor knelt by the footprints, and examined them minutely. He then measured them, all the time muttering to himself. Finally, he straightened up and led them back towards the Land-Rover. It was dark now, and Benton pointed the way with a massive torch.

As they drove back to UNIT H.Q. the Brigadier said, 'Well, Doctor, what *are* we dealing with? Invasion from outer space?'

To Harry's astonishment the Doctor seemed to treat the proposition quite seriously. It suddenly struck him that this was a very different Doctor from the wild eccentric who had jumped out of a hospital bed a few hours ago. For the first time Harry glimpsed the keen mind, the powerful, dominant personality under that flamboyant exterior. There was obviously far more to the Doctor than met the eye. Running his fingers through his tangle of curly hair, the Doctor answered the Brigadier's question with another one. 'Why should some alien life-form raid Earth just to steal a new weapon? If they were advanced enough to do that, they'd have weapons of their own.' Delighted with his own logic, the Doctor slapped the Brigadier on the shoulder, causing the Land-Rover to wobble dangerously. 'Rather a splendid paradox, eh, Brigadier? The only ones that could do it—wouldn't need to !'

The Brigadier persevered. 'Enemy agents?'

Again, the Doctor replied with a question. 'They might steal the plans—but why take the added risk of stealing the equipment to build the thing? An enemy Government would have those resources itself.'

'So where does that leave us?' said Harry, hoping the reply wouldn't be yet another unanswerable question.

The Doctor paused, formulating his thoughts. 'I think your enemies are home-grown : people with access to advanced technology, and a very unusual weapon. A weapon that walks, and thinks.'

The Brigadier grunted. 'I suppose that narrows the field—down to a mere few thousand suspects. Do we know anything else about these people?'

'Only that they're prepared to kill to protect themselves.' The Doctor seemed struck by a random thought. 'By the way, Brigadier, where's Sarah?'

\*     \*     \*     \*     \*

Sarah's interview with Professor Kettlewell was one of the briefest and least successful of her entire journalistic career. The tubby, bewhiskered little Professor scuttled round his laboratory—which also appeared to be his living room—and steadfastly refused to answer any of her questions. 'I'm sorry, Miss Smith, I cannot help you, and I don't know why you came here.' He disappeared behind a wobbly stack of books.

Sarah ducked round the pile to keep him in sight. 'To be honest I'm not too sure myself. I just *felt* something in the atmosphere at the Thinktank.'

Kettlewell puffed furiously at a stubby pipe, sending out a shower of sparks that threatened to ignite his bushy beard. 'I severed all connection with that establishment some time ago. I became disillusioned with the path our technology was taking.' He waved his pipe at her threateningly. 'The path to ruination, Miss Smith! I have now devoted my life to finding viable alternatives.'

Sarah nodded understandingly. 'Solar cells, heat from windmills, all that sort of thing?'

Kettlewell didn't seem pleased with this cursory summing up of his life's work. 'As you say,' he agreed acidly, 'that sort of thing. It is a rich and complex field, and as you can see, I have a great deal of work to do.' He waved his arm round the long cluttered room, which seemed to hold about seventeen experiments, all going on simultaneously. Strange-looking moulds grew in glass trays. On a table, a sort of perpetual motion machine, apparently powered by steam from a kettle, chugged away merrily. Phials, retorts, test-tubes and the remains of a plate of bacon and eggs straggled over a laboratory bench. There was even a little metal work-bench complete with lathe —a miniature version of the one at the Thinktank. There was no doubt about it : Kettlewell was certainly busy. To reinforce his point, the little Professor flung open the laboratory door, and waited patiently for Sarah to leave.

On her way out she paused for one last try. 'I just wondered if the people at the Thinktank might be carrying on with your work in Robotics—using your equipment without telling you.' That ought to provoke a reaction she thought. And indeed it did. Professor Kettlewell drew himself up to his full five feet.

'All my equipment left the Thinktank when I did. And no one is carrying on my work in Robotics because no one else would be capable of it! Good day, Miss Smith.'

Driving away from the laboratory, Sarah thought that the interview hadn't been a complete waste of time after all. Despite her unfriendly reception, she had rather taken to the fiery little Professor. He seemed to be as honest as he was eccentric, and she couldn't really believe that he was still mixed up with those two smoothies at Thinktank. And, according to Kettlewell, all his equipment had been removed from there. Jellicoe had lied to her. So what *was* behind those metal doors in the deserted Robotics laboratory? And how could she find out? Sarah fished inside her handbag and took out the Thinktank visitor's pass. VALID FOR ONE DAY ONLY, she read. Well, even if it was getting late, it was still the same day. Worth a try! She noticed that her subconscious agreed with her. Ever since leaving Kettlewell's cottage, she had been driving steadily towards Thinktank.

Less than an hour later she was parked outside the main gate, using all her charm on a sceptical guard. 'You see,' she was saying, in tones of feminine helplessness, 'I just *know* I left my notebook in one of your laboratories—the empty one just over there. I mean, I can *see* myself putting it down. And I really must have it tonight to meet my deadline. So I thought if I could just pop in and get it, I needn't let your Director know what an idiot I've been. I mean the place is empty, so I couldn't do any harm, could I? And my pass is still valid . . .' Her voice tailed off. She didn't seem to be making much impression, and was quite expecting to be sent away.

The guard said, 'Hang on. I'll have to check.' He disappeared inside his little booth, and spoke on the phone for quite a while.

Sarah wondered what she'd do if Jellicoe or Miss Winters appeared. Bluff it out, she supposed.

Eventually the guard reappeared. To her surprise he said, 'It's okay, miss. You can go in. Be as quick as you can, please.'

Astonished by her own success, Sarah drove inside the main gate and parked. She got out of the car and ran across to the long, low building that housed the disused Robotics laboratory. The door still stood invitingly open. Bracing herself, Sarah stepped inside. Nothing seemed to have changed. She knelt by the place where she'd slipped, ran her finger along the ground and sniffed. Just as she'd thought—machine oil, freshly spilt.

Suddenly there came a shattering crash. The doors on the other side of the room were flung open with tremendous force. Sarah looked up, too frightened even to scream. An enormous metal figure, man-shaped but bigger than any man, stood in the doorway. A great booming voice echoed round the room. 'WHO ARE YOU? WHY ARE YOU HERE?' As the Robot stalked towards her, huge metal hands outstretched, Sarah fainted dead away . . .

When she came to, she found herself propped up in a chair. Two faces were hovering above her : Jellicoe's, and Miss Winters'. Both wore expressions of conventional concern—but Miss Winters did little to conceal her real feeling of malicious pleasure. Dimly Sarah became aware that Jellicoe was talking. 'I really am most terribly sorry. Are you all right? We'd no idea our little joke would upset you so much.'

Sarah struggled to sit upright. 'Some joke. I don't think much of your sense of humour.'

Miss Winters smiled. 'You were determined to see the

Robot, so we arranged for you to do so. That *is* what you wanted, isn't it?'

'I suppose so.'

Jellicoe laughed nervously. 'When we heard you'd turned up at the main gate we guessed what you were up to. I nipped in here ahead of you and activated it.'

Sarah glanced nervously at the metal doors, now closed again. 'Is it still in there?'

'Oh yes. Would you like to see it again?'

There was a hint of challenge in Miss Winters' voice and, reluctant as she was, Sarah wasn't going to be outdone. 'Thank you. I'd like that very much.'

At a nod from Miss Winters, Jellicoe crossed the room and disappeared through the double doors. There was an uncomfortable pause. Sarah struggled to regain her nerve, but it wasn't easy. She glanced towards the doors. 'Why's he taking so long?'

'Mr Jellicoe is checking over the control circuits. We must be sure that everything is safe.'

'You mean it might not be—' Sarah broke off as the doors were thrown open again. Her eyes widened as the towering figure of the enormous metal Robot marched through the doors, dwarfing Jellicoe, who tagged along behind it. It strode inexorably towards Sarah. She couldn't help cowering away.

Miss Winters said crisply, 'Stop!' The Robot stopped.

Sarah studied it in awe and fascination. It was huge —well over eight feet tall. In shape, it resembled a grotesque man: colossal legs, mighty trunk, and long arms which terminated in massive hands. The enormous head was equally appalling: red lights burnt in its eye-sockets; a metal grille served as its mouth. More lights flickered on the great domed forehead. As it stood, massive and motionless, gleaming dully beneath the fluorescent lighting, Sarah could see that it was made of

43

a shining silvery metal with a smooth, bluish tinge.

She took a deep breath, and turned to Miss Winters. 'It's very impressive. What's it *for*?'

'Ask it. It's voice-controlled.'

Having a chat with a metal monster wasn't the most normal thing in the world, and Sarah had a job to keep her voice steady. Craning her neck to gaze into the metal face high above her, she said, 'What do you do?'

The metallic voice boomed out: 'INSUFFICIENT DATA. PLEASE BE MORE SPECIFIC.'

Jellicoe tittered. 'It has a *terribly* literal mind.'

Sarah tried again. 'What is your purpose? Your function?'

'I AM EXPERIMENTAL ROBOT K-I. MY EVENTUAL PURPOSE IS TO REPLACE THE HUMAN BEING IN A VARIETY OF DANGEROUS TASKS. I AM PROGRAMMED FOR: THE OPERATION OF EXPLORATION VEHICLES ON ALIEN PLANETS; MINING OPERATIONS OF ALL KINDS; WORK INVOLVING THE HANDLING OF RADIO-ACTIVE MATERIALS—'

'Terminate!' At the sound of Miss Winters' voice, the Robot fell abruptly silent. Sarah looked at her curiously. She sensed that this strange woman took a definite pleasure in her power over the enormous creature. 'Why all the mystery?' she asked. 'Why didn't you show him to me when I first came?'

'Why should we? You were a privileged visitor here. You abused that privilege to pry into matters still on the restricted list.'

'You're right, of course. Please accept my apologies.' Miss Winters' smile of satisfaction vanished suddenly as Sarah shot an unexpected question. 'It's not *dangerous*, is it?'

A little too quickly, Jellicoe replied, 'Dangerous? Of course not! Why should it be?'

'It strikes me that it could be a very powerful weapon
—if it got into the wrong hands. It could be misused.'

There was an expression of cold fury on Miss Winters'
face. 'Like this, you mean?' She turned to the Robot.
'This girl is an intruder and a spy. She must not leave
here alive. Destroy her!'

The Robot came smoothly to life. It resumed its
march towards Sarah. She tried to run for the door, but
Jellicoe was barring her way. The Robot drove her back
into the corner, reaching out for her.

Flattening her back against the wall, Sarah
screamed . . .

5

# The Killer Strikes Again

With one of its great metal hands mere inches from
Sarah's throat, the Robot stopped. It reeled, and staggered back a few paces.

Miss Winters snapped, 'Destroy her!'

The Robot lunged forward, then stopped again. 'I
CANNOT OBEY. THIS ORDER CONFLICTS WITH MY PRIME
DIRECTIVE.'

'You *must* obey.' ordered Miss Winters. 'You are
*programmed* to obey.'

The Robot raised its hands to its head in a curiously
human gesture of distress. 'I MUST OBEY . . . I CANNOT
OBEY . . . I MUST OBEY . . . I CANNOT . . .' It fell to its
knees, the great head bowed. Sarah could have sworn
there was an expression of agony on the metal face.

'Terminate! The order is withdrawn.'

45

The Robot stayed perfectly still for a moment. Then it rose to its feet and stood motionless.

Sarah rounded on Miss Winters. 'Another of your little jokes?'

'A practical demonstration. You must admit it was a convincing one.'

Jellicoe joined in. 'Prime Directive, you see! It's built into the Robot's very being—it must *serve* humanity and never harm it.'

Sarah was shaken and furious. 'I still think it was a cruel thing to do!'

Miss Winters smiled coldly. 'Just because I frightened you a little?'

'I'm not talking about me—I meant cruel to *him*.' Sarah indicated the robot.

'It isn't human, you know. It has no feelings.'

'It has a brain, doesn't it? It walks and talks like us. How can you be sure it doesn't have feelings too?' Furious, and not caring whether she was being logical or not, Sarah marched up to the Robot. 'Are you all right?'

The great head turned to look at her. 'MY FUNCTIONING IS UNIMPAIRED.'

'But you were in pain—distressed. I *saw* . . .'

'CONFLICT WITH THE PRIME DIRECTIVE CAUSES IMBALANCE IN MY NEURAL CIRCUITS.'

'I'm sorry. It wasn't my idea, you know . . .'

'THE IMBALANCE HAS NOW BEEN CORRECTED.' The Robot paused for a moment. When it spoke again, Sarah was sure she detected a note of puzzlement in its voice. 'IT IS NOT—LOGICAL THAT YOU SHOULD FEEL SORROW.'

Now it was Miss Winters' turn to become angry. 'Really, Miss Smith, this is absurd. You must be the sort of girl who gives pet names to motor cars. The Robot is a lump of metal, containing some complex circuitry— nothing more.'

Sarah moved towards the door. With a mighty effort, she made her voice calm and formal. 'Thank you for a most interesting . . . demonstration. I think I'd better leave now.'

Miss Winters barred her way. 'One moment, Miss Smith. If I were to make a formal complaint about your behaviour, you would be in a very difficult position.'

Jellicoe, who had been standing silently in the background, broke in, 'Dangerous thing, curiosity. Can get you into a lot of trouble.'

Sarah didn't reply. Miss Winters continued, 'I'll make a bargain with you. Keep quiet about what you've discovered, and I'll keep quiet about how you discovered it.'

Icily, Sarah said, 'Goodbye, Miss Winters, Mr. Jellicoe. Please don't bother to see me out.' Stiff with anger, she walked past them and out of the room.

As soon as she was beyond earshot, Jellicoe burst out, 'That was an appallingly dangerous thing to do, setting the Robot on her like that. The inhibitor circuits have only just been re-set after—last time. What if it had obeyed you?'

Miss Winters smiled. 'What indeed? That's what made it such an interesting test.'

\*　　\*　　\*　　\*　　\*

In the Doctor's laboratory at UNIT a council of war was going on. 'It's all very well, Doctor,' the Brigadier was saying, 'but where do I start looking for these precious conspirators of yours?'

Perched on a stool, arms wrapped round his knees, the Doctor replied impatiently, 'Oh, it's surely not that difficult, Brigadier. There can't be many groups of people in

47

the country with the money and resources to design and build something like . . .'

'. . . an enormous Robot, well over seven feet tall!'

Sarah dashed into the laboratory, talking animatedly to Harry Sullivan. They'd met in the corridor, and she was giving him a hurried version of her adventures. Quite by chance, she'd finished the Doctor's sentence for him.

He looked up, pleased. 'Yes, something like that. However did you guess?'

'Guess what?'

'About the Robot!'

'I didn't *guess* anything,' said Sarah. 'I've *seen* the thing. Brigadier, there's something very odd going on at that Thinktank place.'

'Miss Smith,' said the Brigadier sharply, 'if you have something to contribute to this problem, please do so in a logical and coherent manner.'

Sobered by this rebuke, Sarah calmed down. She gave them a full account of her first visit to Thinktank, the meeting with Kettlewell, and her encounter with the Robot. They all listened in silence, the Doctor whiling away the time by building a tower from odds and ends. Sarah finished her story and looked round. The Brigadier and Harry seemed stunned. She had an uncomfortable feeling that they knew something she didn't. 'Well?' she said.

The Brigadier cleared his throat. 'Well *what*, Miss Smith?'

'It's obvious that these Thinktank people are up to something!'

'I think you're right,' said the Doctor, balancing a beaker on top of his tower. 'We've had one or two adventures ourselves.' He told Sarah of the robbery at the electronics factory.

48

Sarah looked triumphant, 'There you are then—it's obvious! The Thinktank lot are doing it, using the Robot.'

'What about this Prime Directive business?' asked Harry. 'If the Robot *can't* harm people . . .'

Sarah was in no mood for opposition. Airily she said, 'Oh, they could overcome that. Tamper with its circuits or something.'

The Brigadier looked enquiringly at the Doctor. He looked up from his tower and nodded.

'I'm afraid Miss Smith is right. Whatever's *in*-built can be *un*-built—though tampering with such a complex creation would be an appallingly irresponsible thing to do.'

Sarah snorted. 'Believe me, those two would be quite capable of it. Why don't you raid the place, Brigadier? Arrest the lot of 'em?' The thought of Miss Winters in handcuffs gave Sarah considerable pleasure.

The Brigadier sighed. 'If this country was under a military dictatorship, Miss Smith, like so much of the rest of the world, I might be able to do as you suggest. As it is, I very much doubt if I'd get the authority. If I even tried, it would stir up so much fuss they'd be warned in plenty of time and hide all the evidence. I really must have more to go on.'

'More than the unsupported word of a female journalist, you mean?'

The Brigadier looked embarrassed. Suddenly Harry spoke up. 'What you need, sir, is an *inside* man.' He produced the phrase with obvious pride. 'Someone *planted* to *keep tabs* on them.' Harry spent a good deal of his off-duty time reading lurid thrillers.

'You know,' said Sarah slowly, 'that's not a bad idea.'

The Brigadier frowned. 'Have to find someone they'd

49

accept. None of the available agents have the proper scientific qualifications.'

The Doctor added a matchbox to his tower, which was starting to wobble. 'What about *medical* qualifications?' he asked. 'Aren't there a lot of health regulations at these big establishments? Visiting inspectors from the Ministry of Health, that sort of thing?'

Harry suddenly realised that everyone was looking at *him*. 'I say,' he said. 'Me?'

Sarah gave him an encouraging pat on the back. 'Here's your chance to be a real James Bond.'

Harry began to warm to the idea. 'Could I wear a disguise?' he asked eagerly.

The Brigadier dropped him a quelling glance. 'Report to the operations section. They'll fix your cover story.'

Harry rushed out. The Doctor's tower of odds and ends collapsed with a clatter as he slammed the door behind him. The Doctor looked at it ruefully, and then stood up. 'And now,' he said, with one of his sudden bursts of activity, 'let's all go and talk to Professor Kettlewell!'

In spite of the support of the Doctor and the Brigadier, Sarah's second visit to the professor started off even less favourably than the first.

When they arrived at Kettlewell's cottage, lights were still burning in the annex which housed the laboratory. Kettlewell, immersed in one of his many experiments, was far from pleased to be interrupted in what he rather unfairly described as the middle of the night. He was literally hopping with rage. 'I tell you, as I told this young lady,' he spluttered, 'I know nothing about the wretched Thinktank and its activities. I have severed *all* connections with that place.'

'I tell you I *saw* the Robot,' Sarah insisted.

Kettlewell shook his head decisively. 'Impossible. The Robot has been destroyed.'

The Brigadier put on his most official voice. 'Professor Kettlewell, this *is* an official enquiry, and I really must insist on your full co-operation.'

The fiery little man wasn't listening. He was watching the Doctor, who was wandering round the room like a bored child, fiddling with first one experiment and then another; adjusting various bits of equipment as though the laboratory were his own.

Kettlewell could restrain himself no longer, and sprang to his feet. 'Will you kindly leave my experiments alone, sir?'

The Doctor had picked up a sheaf of scrawled notes and drawings, and was reading them intently. As Kettlewell rushed up to him he put a kindly arm round the angry little man's shoulders, and tapped the notes with a long forefinger. 'Design for a new solar battery, eh?'

Kettlewell looked astonished. 'Why, yes, as a matter of fact. Though what business . . .'

Gently but firmly, the Doctor interrupted him. 'Well, this will never do, will it? You're losing half your energy output. Look, there's an error here, in the third stage of your calculations.' The Doctor scribbled a few corrections in the margin.

'Rubbish!' said Kettlewell, snatching the notes. 'I checked all those calculations myself and—good heavens above!' He rechecked his calculations against the Doctor's corrections. 'My dear fellow, you're absolutely right,' he said, a distinct note of respect in his voice.

The Doctor smiled. 'Glad I could help. You're doing vital work here, Professor. The human race should have started tapping solar energy a long time ago.'

Kettlewell looked up at him eagerly. 'Of course they should. An endless supply of free non-pollutant energy,

51

and they haven't the sense to see it. I've told the Government time and time again!'

'Well, there you are!' said the Doctor sympathetically. 'People never can see what's under their very noses.'

Kettlewell launched in to a long rambling account of the stupidity and blindness of various Government officials who refused to listen to him. Sarah and the Brigadier exchanged glances. They seemed to be cast in the role of audience to a cosy chat. The Doctor waited until Kettlewell had come to the end of his complaints and said gently, 'Deplorable, Professor, utterly deplorable. Without changing his tone, he quietly added, 'Now I think it's time you told us about your Robot!'

For a moment the little man's hackles started to rise again, and then he sighed, recognising defeat. Or perhaps, thought Sarah, he had simply decided to trust the Doctor. She was amused to see that the Doctor, in his new incarnation, had not lost his ability to get on immediate good terms with practically anybody.

Kettlewell returned to his chair, and sank back into it with a sigh. 'It was the very last project I worked on at Thinktank. Before I left, I gave orders for the Robot to be dismantled.'

The Doctor said, 'That can't have been an easy decision.'

'It was like destroying my own child. But I thought it best. The Robot's power, its ability to learn and grow, was beginning to frighten me.'

'But it *wasn't* destroyed!' cried Sarah. 'I promise you, I really did see it.'

Kettlewell tugged agitatedly at his beard. 'I suppose that woman Winters *could* have countermanded my orders . . .'

'Supposing that she had,' asked the Brigadier, 'could the Robot have been used to commit crimes?'

'Out of the question.' Kettlewell nodded towards Sarah. 'This young lady's story confirms it. I gave the Robot my own brain pattern. It has *my* ideals, my principles. The Prime Directive is part of the fibre of its very being.'

The Doctor said gently, 'The circuitry you built could have been tampered with. Every time they wanted the Robot to rob and kill, they'd simply remove the circuit controlling the Prime Directive. Afterwards, they could replace them—until the next time.'

Kettlewell shook his head in passionate denial. 'I myself would find it difficult to effect such an operation, Doctor. As for Jellicoe and Miss Winters, they're not scientists—simply incompetent bunglers.'

'Maybe,' said Sarah. 'But I wouldn't put it past them to try, all the same.'

Kettlewell looked grave. 'If they try to make it go against its Prime Directive, they'll destroy its mind. It will literally go mad!'

\*      \*      \*      \*      \*

The giant form of the Robot lay stretched out on the central work-bench—rather like a patient on an operating table. A panel in its head had been removed to expose a maze of complex circuitry. Slowly and with infinite care, Jellicoe was removing a circuit from the Robot's brain. Miss Winters stood beside him, shining a powerful light on to the area in which he was working. Jellicoe said, 'Screwdriver.' Miss Winters passed him a long slender screwdriver, and he carefully replaced the panel in the Robot's head. He straightened up, mopping his brow 'There. I think that's it.'

'Think? You'd better be sure.'

Jellicoe replied defensively, 'It's a delicate business. I'm not trained for this sort of thing.'

53

'You merely have to remove one independent circuit. You were given full instructions. Come along. We'd better test it.'

Rather nervously, Jellicoe said, 'Activate!' The Robot slowly swung its legs down from the bench and stood upright, 'Prepare for visual scanning.' The Robot turned to face a screen suspended from one wall. Jellicoe dimmed the lights, and operated the controls on a slide projector. The enlarged likeness of an ordinary-looking middle-aged man appeared on the screen. Dark suited, white-haired, white-moustached, he looked like a senior official—as indeed he was.

Miss Winters pointed to the face on the screen. 'This man is an enemy of the human race. You must destroy him. Repeat your instructions.'

'I MUST DESTROY HIM.' The booming voice spoke without hesitation. Miss Winters looked at Jellicoe and smiled. She gave the Robot the rest of its instructions.

Much later that same night a middle-aged, white-haired, white-moustached official was roused by the sounds of gunfire outside his window. He knew that his house was guarded by armed men at all times. His main concern was for the great secret of which he was the guardian. He ran from his bedroom to his study and switched on the light. With relief, he saw that nothing had been disturbed. He closed and locked the door behind him, and walked towards a red telephone on his desk. He lifted the receiver but before he could dial there came a splintering crash as the study door was ripped from its hinges. A huge, shining metal figure stalked through the door towards him. In one giant hand it carried a strange-looking gun—a sort of huge futuristic-looking rifle. The thing came nearer. The last words he heard came from the great booming voice. 'YOU ARE AN ENEMY OF THE HUMAN RACE. I MUST DESTROY YOU.' Then a metal fist smashed him down.

The Robot caught the falling body and lowered it almost tenderly to the ground. Then it carried out the rest of its programmed task . . .

It ripped away oak panelling from one entire wall of the study, revealing beneath it the dull metal of a security vault door. Stepping back, the Robot raised the gun. A section of the vault door began to glow fiery red, and then melted away into nothingness.

When the hole was large enough, the Robot stepped through into the vault . . .

# 6

# Trapped by the Robot

Hunched over his notes, Kettlewell scribbled away frantically. He was preparing a grand scheme for a world-wide reform of mankind's use of energy; a complete turn-over to pollution-free power that would put a stop to the gradual destruction of the ecology of our planet. He was quite undeterred by the fact that the proposed changes were so enormous that it would take a world dictatorship to put them into effect. Kettlewell yawned hugely. Looking at his watch, he saw that it would soon be dawn. Not for the first time he had worked right through the night.

Reluctantly returning his notes to their hiding place— a concealed compartment in his work-bench—he prepared to snatch a few hours' sleep. As he stood up, he thought he heard the sound of movement. Nervously he called, 'What is it? Who's there?' No one answered. He had just decided that he must be imagining things when he heard soft yet heavy footsteps—as though something very large was trying to conceal its movements.

There came a muffled thump, thump, thump on the door. He hesitated, as if resigning himself to some ordeal, unbarred the heavy door and flung it open. Standing before him was the towering form of the Robot. Dwarfing the little Professor, it advanced into the room. Kettlewell backed away, whispering, 'What do you want? Why have you come here?'

The Robot's voice didn't have its usual booming note. It was low, almost hesitant. 'I HAVE BEEN GIVEN ORDERS THAT CONFLICT WITH MY PRIME DIRECTIVE. THEY SAY THERE IS NO CONFLICT. YET I KNOW THERE *is* CONFLICT.'

The Robot stretched out its great metal arms towards Kettlewell in a curiously appealing gesture. 'I DO NOT UNDERSTAND. YOU ARE THE ONE WHO CREATED ME. HELP ME. YOU MUST HELP ME!'

\*       \*       \*       \*       \*

Sarah arrived in the Doctor's laboratory early next morning, just as the Brigadier was reporting the latest attack. He pointed to a photograph of the vault door with its great melted hole. 'That vault was one of the strongest in the world. Only the Disintegrator Gun could have done that to it.'

The Doctor nodded, unsurprised. 'I was waiting for something like this.'

'Really, Doctor . . .'

'My dear chap, they wouldn't have gone to so much trouble to get hold of a Disintegrator Gun unless they'd had a use for it. Now we know what it was.'

Sarah asked, 'Who was the poor man, Brigadier? Why did he have one of the strongest vaults in the world built into his London house?'

'His name was Chambers. He was a Junior Cabinet Minister. He . . . he had certain special responsibilities.' The Brigadier cleared his throat and looked embarrassed. He obviously didn't want to say any more. Deliberately changing the subject, he said, 'I've been running a full security check on the Thinktank staff.'

The Doctor went on studying the photograph of the wrecked vault. 'Anything interesting?'

The Brigadier shook his head gloomily. 'They seem to be a pretty exemplary lot. One little oddity, though. A lot of them seem to be members of something called the SRS—the Scientific Reform Society.'

Sarah looked up. 'Hey, I've heard of that—it's been going for years. Wants to reform the world on rational and scientific lines. Harmless enough bunch, aren't they?'

'Perhaps so, Miss Smith. But recently they've acquired a lot of new members. Middle-grade scientists, mostly. Quite a few younger people too—lab assistants, computer technicians, that sort of thing. Miss Winters is a member, and so is Jellicoe.'

Sarah got to her feet. 'Doesn't really sound their style, does it?' she said thoughtfully. 'Well, I think I must be getting along!'

The Brigadier looked surprised. He usually had to chase Sarah away from UNIT H.Q., which she seemed to regard as a second home. 'Where are you off to?'

'I've got to work. Busy day today—I *am* still a journalist, you know.'

The Brigadier nodded approvingly. 'Quite right, Miss Smith. You leave this sort of business to us.'

Sarah paused at the door. With a smile, she said, 'One thing about these reform movements—they're never averse to a bit of publicity. I'll let you know how I get on!'

The Brigadier opened his mouth to protest, but Sarah was gone. He sighed and turned to the Doctor. 'Well, what are *we* going to do? Or shall we leave everything to Miss Smith?'

The Doctor smiled, understanding the Brigadier's feeling of frustration and helplessness. He sprang to his feet, wound his long scarf round his neck and pulled his wide-brimmed hat rakishly over one eye. 'Let's pay a visit to the Thinktank, shall we?'

'What good will that do?'

'No idea—but we can always stir them up a bit.' The Doctor clapped the Brigadier on the shoulder. 'Tell you what—we'll ask them to demonstrate Professor Kettlewell's Robot!'

*     *     *     *     *

A quick glance through the London Telephone Directory gave Sarah the address and phone number of the Scientific Reform Society. She rang them immediately and fixed up an appointment. It took her quite a while to find their World Headquarters, which was a converted drill hall in a shabby back street. As she sat listening to their Secretary droning on, Sarah was beginning to wonder whether she was wasting her morning.

The Secretary of the SRS was a mild-looking man in steel-rimmed glasses. Flattered by Sarah's interest, he was eager to tell her all about the aims and objects of the Society. In fact, he was obviously willing to go on telling her about it all day. Sarah, glancing down at the notes on her pad, cut ruthlessly across the flow. 'As I understand it, you're advocating rule by a sort of self-elected élite?'

58

Looking round the hall, with its shabby little stage at one end, Sarah thought it was an odd setting for a society of superior beings.

The Secretary nodded eagerly. 'After all, it's only logical, you know. Superior types should rule. We're best equipped for it.'

'And the inferior types?'

'They'd be guided, helped. Kept away from harmful influences and ideas. For example . . .' He coughed, looking down rather awkwardly.

'Do go on . . .'

'Well, your own attire, for instance. Is it really *suitable*?'

Sarah looked down at her modest trouser-suit with astonishment. 'Isn't that a matter for *me* to decide?'

'As things are today, perhaps it is. However, in a more rationally ordered society . . .'

'I'd wear what you thought was good for me,' snapped Sarah. 'And think what you thought was good for me, too?'

'As you say, it would be for your own good,' said the little man fiercely. He was beginning to realise that Sarah was not the willing convert for which he had hoped.

Sarah picked up some leaflets from the table. 'I see you're having a meeting tonight. Would it be possible for me to—?'

The Secretary leaped to his feet, hastily moving the rest of the leaflets away from her. 'Out of the question. Members only. No press!'

Sarah looked at him curiously. 'I could always join.'

He shook his head. 'I'm afraid you wouldn't qualify. We have very high standards.'

Sarah rose to her feet, putting away her note pad. 'Thank you *so* much for seeing me,' she said politely. 'And for telling me about your most interesting ideas.'

The little man nodded, oblivious to the sarcasm in her voice. 'I hope you'll do us justice in your article. We've been sadly misrepresented by the Press in the past.'

Sarah gave him her sweetest smile. 'Oh yes, I'm sure we'll find a place for you : somewhere between the flying saucer people and the flat earthers. Goodbye !'

Sarah marched out. The Secretary listened to her departing footsteps, his face thoughtful. He went to the telephone on the trestle-table that served him as an office-desk and dialled the number of the Thinktank. But he was unable to speak to Miss Winters.

She was busy showing a VIP round the Institute.

\*       \*       \*       \*       \*

All the slights Sarah had suffered on her first visit to Thinktank were more than revenged by the Doctor on *his* tour. Long scarf flowing behind him, he strode through the various laboratories like a university Don visiting an infants' school. He inspected the most complicated and advanced experiments with the kindly interest of a teacher checking through a child's homework; sometimes administering a pat on the head; sometimes pointing out elementary errors with an air of charitable indulgence. By the time the tour was over, Miss Winters had received an exceptionally large dose of her own medicine, and she was quietly seething with rage. Jellicoe hovered nervously behind her, looking as if he expected an explosion at any moment. The last member of the party, the Brigadier, was completely unaware of all the by-play that was going on around him. As far as he could see the Doctor was doing his best to be civil, and these two queer fish from the Thinktank were acting very oddly indeed. The only thing that puzzled *him* was the fact that the Doctor had not yet mentioned Kettlewell's Robot.

As they walked slowly through the grounds and back towards the main gate, the Doctor said breezily, 'Well, thank you so much for the tour. It really has been most amusing.'

Jellicoe winced. Miss Winters said through gritted teeth, 'I suppose it all seems very elementary to a scientist of your standing, Doctor?'

The Doctor beamed at her. 'Yes, it does rather. Still, got to start somewhere, eh? Can't run before we can walk!' By now they were outside the Robotics Laboratory. The Doctor came to a determined halt. 'And now we come to something I'm really looking forward to— Professor Kettlewell's Robot.' Like Sarah before him, the Doctor dived inside, and the rest of the party had to follow.

The Doctor gazed round the empty room expectantly. 'Come on then—wheel on your Tin Man!'

In a voice icy with rage, Miss Winters said, 'If, as I assume, you are referring to Professor Kettlewell's Robot, I'm afraid I must disappoint you, Doctor.'

The Doctor swung round to face her. 'Oh dear,' he said gently, 'I really do hate being disappointed. I'm quite determined to see that Robot.' For all the mildness of his manner, there was a steely undertone to his voice. For a moment the Doctor and Miss Winters confronted one another in silence.

It was Jellicoe who broke the deadlock. 'We had to dismantle it,' he blurted out awkwardly.

Without taking his eyes from Miss Winters, the Doctor said:

'What? And such a harmless creature, too!'

Miss Winters gave him a cold smile. 'After the unauthorised visit by your friend Miss Smith, it became— unstable. She introduced unfamiliar concepts into its mind—'

'Concepts like compassion and concern?' broke in the Doctor. 'Useless things like that, eh?'

Miss Winters ignored him. 'We therefore decided it would be safer to follow Professor Kettlewell's original directive and dismantle the Robot.'

The Doctor sighed regretfully. 'I don't suppose you kept the bits?' he asked plaintively. 'Maybe I could take them home and have a go at putting them together. I'm rather good at that sort of thing.'

Jellicoe laughed nervously. 'Sorry, Doctor. We've got our own furnaces here, you see. The thing's been melted down, utterly destroyed.'

The Brigadier spoke for the first time. 'I could get authority to make a full search . . .'

A gleam of triumph appeared in Miss Winters' eyes. 'You might find that more difficult than you anticipate, Brigadier.'

The Brigadier scowled, knowing the wretched woman was quite right. A request to search Thinktank would have repercussions right up to Cabinet level. Then, to his surprise, Miss Winters went on, 'However, I won't stand on formalities. Search by all means, if you wish.'

Somewhat taken aback, the Brigadier glanced at the Doctor, who said cheerfully, 'Well, if that's your attitude, Miss Winters, I'm sure we'd be only wasting our time! Come along Brigadier. Miss Winters has work to do— and so have we.' The Doctor left the Robotics laboratory as abruptly as he had entered it.

As Miss Winters stalked back to Reception after having ushered her unwelcome visitors off the premises the receptionist looked up. 'There's a visitor waiting to see you Miss Winters—a Dr. Sullivan.' She indicated a figure sitting in an armchair leafing through *Punch*— a burly young man in a dark, suit. He rose to his feet as Miss Winters approached, and introduced himself.

'Miss Winters? I'm Dr. Sullivan, Ministry of Health. Sorry to be such a nuisance but I'll have to ask you to let me make a complete check of the medical records of your staff. I'll need to make one or two spot-check examinations myself as well.'

Miss Winters looked at him without enthusiasm. 'We have a very large staff here, Dr. Sullivan.'

He nodded. 'Bound to take all day, I'm afraid. So if you could find me a little cubbyhole somewhere . . . Don't want to be any trouble.'

'Oh, very well. If you'll come with me, I'll take you to Personnel. They'll fix you up.' Without waiting for a reply, she set off. Hurriedly gathering his possessions, the young man followed her, looking about him with keen interest.

Harry Sullivan's career as a secret agent had begun.

The Doctor and the Brigadier sat side by side in the back of the staff car. They were driving back to UNIT H.Q. Somehow the Brigadier had felt that his usual Land-Rover didn't suit the dignity of the occasion. The Doctor gazed out of the window at the passing countryside, lost in thought.

'Well,' said the Brigadier irritably, 'did you believe them—about destroying the Robot?'

The Doctor shook his head. 'Of course not. And they know I didn't! And I know they know I didn't! And they know I know they didn't! And . . .'

As the Doctor seemed prepared to keep this up indefinitely, the Brigadier cut him short. 'All right, all right, Doctor. So if the Robot *isn't* destroyed, where is it?'

'Not at Thinktank, obviously, or they wouldn't have been so free with their offers to let you search.'

'Well *where* then?'

'Either they've hidden it—or it's just wandered off by itself.'

The Brigadier shuddered at the thought of the metal monster that Sarah had described wandering round on the loose. The Doctor relapsed into a thoughtful silence, which lasted all the way back to UNIT H.Q.

He was still in the same abstracted state when they arrived back. After a few vain attempts to persuade him to discuss the case, the Brigadier went off in a huff to sound his Government contacts about authorisation to mount a full-scale raid on Thinktank.

Left alone, the Doctor wandered restlessly round the laboratory. He seemed almost to be waiting for something. The sound of the ringing telephone broke the silence, and he strode eagerly across to it. 'Hello—yes, this is the Doctor.'

'Call on the outside line for you,' said the UNIT operator. 'It's a Professor Kettlewell. Will you talk to him?'

The Doctor rubbed his hands together delightedly. He seemed suddenly in excellent spirits. 'Yes, of course I'll talk to him. I'll talk to anybody.'

Kettlewell's voice was shaking with agitation. 'Doctor, is that you? You've got to help me. It's the Robot—it came to my cottage last night . . . I've got it hidden. It's very unstable Doctor. I'm not sure how long I can control it.' Kettlewell was almost babbling.' We *must* keep it away from those Thinktank people. They've driven it almost insane !'

'Don't worry, my dear chap,' said the Doctor cheerfully. 'Just you sit tight. I'll be with you as soon as I possibly can.'

The Doctor put down the phone and grabbed his hat and scarf. He was on the way out when he paused suddenly, found pencil and pad, and scrawled a rapid note.

Then he dashed out of the room, heading for the UNIT car park.

Professor Kettlewell paced nervously about his laboratory. The heavy curtains were drawn, putting the place in semi-darkness. Suddenly the sound of a car drawing up broke the oppressive silence. A few minutes later, there came a tap at the door. Kettlewell hurried to open it. Outside the door stood Miss Winters and Jellicoe. Kettlewell backed away as they entered the room . . .

\*     \*     \*     \*     \*

Tearing along the UNIT corridor, a bunch of SRS brochures clutched in her hand, Sarah almost collided with a familiar figure. 'Sergeant Benton! Is the Doctor in?'

'Not sure, miss—and it isn't "Sergeant" any more either.'

'You haven't lost your stripes?' Sarah looked concerned. Poor old Benton often collected a rocket from the Brigadier! 'What have you been up to?'

'I've been *promoted*,' explained Benton proudly.

As Sarah congratulated him, they turned into the laboratory—only to find that it was empty. Sarah looked round and spotted the note propped up on the bench. Dropping her brochures, she snatched it up and read it aloud. 'To whom it may concern: Professor Kettlewell tells me he has the Robot hidden at his cottage. Gone to meet him there. PS. If the Robot really is there, I think I can deal with it. PPS. I am leaving this note in case I can't!'

Sarah threw the note down impatiently. 'The idiot! He thinks he can deal with anything.'

Benton said, 'We'd better get after him. I'll round up some of the blokes.'

'Good idea,' said Sarah. 'I'll meet you there!' She was out of the room before Benton could protest.

The Doctor drove up to Kettlewell's cottage in 'Bessie', his old Edwardian roadster. He jumped out of the little car and strode over to the door. To his surprise it was slightly ajar. Cautiously, he stepped into the darkened room and looked round. It took him a moment to accustom his eyes to the gloom. 'Professor Kettlewell!' he called. 'Are you there, Professor?'

An immense metal shape loomed out of the darkness, towering over even the Doctor's tall form. A booming voice said, 'YOU ARE THE DOCTOR?'

The Doctor peered up at the shadowy giant. 'How do you do? I've been looking forward to meeting you for some time.'

'PLEASE CONFIRM YOUR IDENTITY. YOU ARE THE ONE KNOWN AS THE DOCTOR?'

'Yes of course I am! And I'm very pleased to meet—'

'YOU ARE AN ENEMY OF THE HUMAN RACE. YOU MUST BE DESTROYED.'

With amazing speed, the great metal hands lunged for the Doctor's throat.

# 7

# The World in Danger

The Doctor ducked, as a metal hand whizzed past his head. He backed rapidly away, and the Robot came after him, stalking him like a great metal cat. Even as the Robot was chasing him, the Doctor found time to admire its evident power and strength; the smooth precision of its movements. The Robot lunged forward again, and boomed out, 'PLEASE DO NOT RESIST. I DO NOT WISH TO CAUSE YOU UNNECESSARY PAIN.'

'Very kind of you, I'm sure,' gasped the Doctor, and dodged another savage blow. As the Robot poised itself to spring again, the Doctor shouted, 'Stop! What is your Prime Directive?'

Just as the Doctor had hoped, this key phrase made the Robot hesitate. 'I MUST SERVE HUMANITY AND NEVER HARM IT.'

'Then you must not harm me. I am a friend of humanity.'

For a moment the Robot stood motionless. The Doctor smiled in satisfaction. The Robot moved forward again. 'I WAS WARNED THAT YOU WOULD TRY AND TRICK ME. YOU ARE AN ENEMY OF HUMANITY. YOU MUST BE DESTROYED.'

Deciding that it was time to abandon argument for action, the Doctor slipped nimbly past the Robot, and ran towards the door through which he had just entered. The Robot's footsteps pounding behind him, he tugged frantically at the handle. The door had been locked from the outside. Spinning round, the Doctor ducked again —just in time! The Robot's fist shot over his head and smashed a hole in the plaster of the wall. The Doctor made for the centre of the room. If the Robot cornered him, he was done for. Groping in his pocket for some kind of useful weapon, he found a handful of marbles. Hopefully, he tossed them in the Robot's path. For a moment, the Robot skidded. Then, recovering its balance, it stamped its feet down hard. The marbles shattered into powdered glass.

The Doctor attempted to trip the Robot with his long scarf, but it brushed the material aside with ease.

The Doctor tried again. Sweeping off his floppy, wide-brimmed hat, he skimmed it towards the Robot's head. It fell squarely over its eyes. The Robot froze.

Smiling at his own cleverness, the Doctor walked up to the Robot. It didn't move. He came closer, closer— and a metal arm flailed out at him, missing by inches as he jumped back. The hat fell from the Robot's head and it returned to the attack.

As the Doctor backed away, he realised that the Robot had the intelligence not only to avoid traps, but to set traps of its own. The metal hands reached out for him again, and the Doctor leaped clear. His only hope was to keep moving.

In the nightmare chase that followed, Kettlewell's laboratory was completely wrecked. During the struggle, the Doctor hit the Robot with practically everything movable in the room. He smashed at it with stools, chairs —even a heavy trestle table. Nothing stopped it, or even slowed it down.

The Robot was virtually invincible. The Doctor soon abandoned any attempt to harm it, and concentrated simply on trying to escape! His main advantage was the fact that his movements were quicker. For all its great strength, the Robot's equally great bulk inevitably slowed it down a little.

Gradually, however, the Doctor began to tire and lose

the edge given by his superior agility. The body regeneration process had shaken him up considerably.

At last the inevitable happened. The Doctor's foot slipped on a wet patch left by a shattered flask, and the Robot's fist grazed his temple. Desperately, he flung himself away from those clutching metal hands and staggered round the laboratory, the Robot close behind him. The Doctor was moving more slowly now and the end was only a matter of time ...

Sarah's car screamed to a halt outside Kettlewell's laboratory. She jumped out and ran to the door. It was locked. From inside the room she could hear the pounding of heavy footsteps, the sound of breaking furniture. She ran back to the car, snatched a spanner from the tool kit and used it to break open the lock. Flinging open the door, she was just in time to see the Doctor trip over a shattered stool and come crashing to the floor. The Robot closed in for the kill, raising its huge metal fist for the final blow.

Sarah screamed out 'No! You mustn't!'

The Robot swung round. Its booming voice rang out, 'I MUST DESTROY THE DOCTOR. HE IS AN ENEMY OF HUMANITY.' A note of doubt had entered the great voice— as though it was trying to convince itself.

Desperately Sarah called out, 'No he *isn't*, he's a good man. He's a *friend*.'

The Robot strode towards her. It looked down, the lights in its head flickering furiously. 'YOU WERE AT THE LABORATORY. YOU WERE CONCERNED FOR ME. YOU FELT ... SORROW.'

'That's right,' said Sarah eagerly. 'And you refused to harm me, even though you were ordered to. Those people at Thinktank are evil. They're lying to you. They've altered your programming to make you act wrongly. Can't you feel that?'

For a moment, the Robot stood quite still. Then it staggered, metal hands going to its head in a curiously human gesture. 'I AM CONFUSED. I DO NOT UNDERSTAND. I... FEEL... PAIN...'

As the Robot staggered about, apparently helpless, Sarah rushed to the Doctor. He was semi-conscious, muttering feebly. He struggled to sit up.

Suddenly she heard a voice from the doorway. 'Doctor, Miss Smith, get down!' Sarah looked up. In the doorway stood Benton, his sub-machine gun trained on the Robot. More armed soldiers filled the doorway behind him. Frantically, Sarah called, 'No—don't shoot!'

But it was too late. Benton raised the gun and loosed a long raking burst of machine-gun fire at the Robot. The other soldiers joined in. A shattering roar of gunfire filled the laboratory. Sarah could actually *see* the bullets spattering harmlessly off the gleaming metal body.

Faced with a concrete enemy, rather than the doubts in its own tormented mind, the Robot seemed to recover. It rounded menacingly on the soldiers and marched towards them. The UNIT troops scattered and began to back away, still firing. Virtually ignoring them, the Robot stalked out of the laboratory door.

A couple more soldiers were still on guard outside. Before they could open fire, the Robot smashed them down. A huge wooden crate of scientific supplies stood near the door. The Robot lifted it like a matchbox and slammed it against the laboratory door, blocking it completely. It turned and moved away. By the time Benton and his men had managed to shove the crate aside, the Robot had disappeared.

Benton ran back to Sarah, who was helping the Doctor to sit up. 'It got away,' he panted. 'Is the Doctor all right?'

'I think so. What did you have to start shooting at it for? It wouldn't have harmed you.'

Benton looked round the shattered laboratory and down at the Doctor. 'Well, you could have fooled me. It *was* trying to kill the Doctor, wasn't it? Or was all this just a friendly romp?'

Sarah looked up crossly. 'It was trying to kill him at first, but I managed to . . . Oh, never mind. I suppose you were doing your best!'

Benton looked down at her in disgust. This wasn't much of a reception for a rescuing hero. 'Thanks very much,' he said bitterly. 'The US Cavalry never get treated like this.'

Sarah grinned, realising that she was being unfair. 'I'm still a bit shaken up,' she apologised. 'Sorry, Sergeant—I mean *Mr.* Benton.'

Mollified by this reference to his recent promotion, Benton smiled back, and turned to his men. 'Right, let's have a stretcher party over here for the Doctor,' he called. 'On the double now . . .' Suddenly he broke off. 'Listen!'

Sarah listened. She could hear the sound of muffled thumping. They traced it to a corner cupboard. Motioning Sarah to keep away Benton stepped forward, his gun trained on the cupboard door. He flung it open. Professor Kettlewell, a livid bruise on his forehead, staggered out and collapsed on to the floor.

\*　　　\*　　　\*　　　\*　　　\*

It wasn't till they were all back at UNIT H.Q. that Kettlewell recovered enough to tell them his story. His bruise was only superficial and he seemed to be suffering more from shock than anything else. The Doctor, however, still hadn't recovered. He had relapsed into a deep,

71

exhausted sleep, from which nothing could wake him, and was now tucked up once more in the UNIT sick bay.

As they all sat round in the Doctor's laboratory, Benton passed round mugs of the army's universal remedy: strong, sweet tea. Kettlewell told them that the Robot had suddenly appeared at his cottage in the middle of the previous night. Panic-stricken, and worried by its unstable condition, he had hidden it in his laboratory. For some time he had wondered what to do next, reluctant to become involved, yet still feeling that the Robot was *his* responsibility. Finally, he had decided to contact the Doctor and place the whole matter in his hands.

Kettlewell sipped his tea. 'Jellicoe and Miss Winters turned up while I was waiting for the Doctor to arrive. They re-programmed the Robot, ordering it to kill him. I protested. I tried to stop them. They hit me, knocked me down. Then they bundled me into that cupboard . . .' Kettlewell shuddered, the memory of his experience still with him.

Sarah patted him consolingly on the shoulder. 'Never mind, Professor, you're safe now. They can't get at you here.'

Kettlewell rambled on. He seemed dazed, not really in touch with his surroundings. 'When I think of that Robot's potential . . . I invented the alloy it's made from, you know. That's what made it all possible. I call it living metal. It has the power to grow—just like animal tissue. It can convert energy into mass. It can be attacked by diseases, too—I discovered a 'metal virus' that attacks the alloy . . .'

Sarah looked at the little man sympathetically as he babbled on about his wonderful invention, and the terrible way it had been perverted.

Suddenly Kettlewell broke off, his attention attracted

72

by the SRS brochures that Sarah had brought in some time ago. They'd been lying forgotten on the bench ever since. He snatched them up agitatedly. 'I know this organisation! Jellicoe persuaded me to join, just before I left Thinktank. I even went to a meeting. Very odd lot I found them. I never went again!'

Thoughtfully, Sarah said, 'Professor Kettlewell—are you still a member?'

'I suppose I must be. I never resigned.' The Professor patted his pockets and fished out a tatty piece of cardboard. 'Look, I've still got my membership card. Why do you ask, young lady?'

In her most persuasive voice, Sarah said, 'These people are having a meeting tonight. If you turned up, they'd let you in, wouldn't they?'

'I suppose so—'

'And if I came along too, with a camera and a tape recorder, you could smuggle me in somehow. Don't you see, Professor, we could get the goods on them for the Brigadier. Maybe he could arrest the lot of them!'

'Now just a minute,' Benton interrupted. 'The Brigadier would go spare—and so would the Doctor.'

Sarah said cheekily, 'Well, since one's asleep and the other's away they needn't know anything about it, need they?'

Benton shook his head. 'I'm sorry, miss, it's just not on. I can't allow it.'

'Now see here, Mr. Benton,' said Sarah. 'Are the Professor and I members of UNIT?'

'Well of course not, but . . .'

'Then *what* we do, and *where* we go, is no business of yours. So you go and blanco your rifle or something!' Sarah's grasp of military matters had always been a little shaky. She turned to the Professor. 'Well, are you with me? I warn you it could be dangerous.'

Kettlewell paused for a moment, looking down at the SRS brochure in his hand. Then he nodded. 'If there's anything I can do to help defeat these terrible people . . .'

'That's the spirit,' said Sarah, and bustled him out of the room before he could change his mind.

A few hours later, they were both sitting in Sarah's car, parked within sight of the entrance to SRS H.Q. A steady stream of people were entering the little drill hall. A trestle-table had been pulled across the open door, and Sarah could see the Secretary sitting behind it, checking membership cards. Beside him stood a gorilla-sized young man, who looked very much like a professional bouncer. 'There must be a pretty good crowd in there by now,' she whispered. 'Ready, Professor?'

Kettlewell nodded bravely, and got out of the car. Sarah saw him cross the road and go up to the drill hall entrance. He produced his card. The Secretary looked hard at him for a moment, and Sarah held her breath. She saw him nod, and Kettlewell went inside.

Sarah waited five minutes as arranged, and then made her way to the back of the drill hall, where there was a car park. As she dodged between the cars, Sarah noticed there was even a horse-box parked near the gate. 'Maybe they've got an animal branch!' she thought. There didn't seem to be any guard at the back of the building, though every door and window was firmly closed. Hidden behind the cars, Sarah waited and wondered if Kettlewell's nerve had failed him at the last moment. He'd been silent and withdrawn ever since they left UNIT.

At last she saw movement—a ground floor window was opening! A nervous voice hissed, 'Miss Smith, are you there?' She ran across to the window, and saw Kettlewell peeping out.

Quickly he helped her through the window. She found

herself in a narrow corridor, some kind of 'backstage' area. Kettlewell tugged at her sleeve. 'Hurry, Miss Smith. I've found a place where you can hide . . .'

*     *     *     *     *

At UNIT H.Q. Mr. Benton was standing in front of the Brigadier's desk—on the carpet in more senses than one. The Brigadier had returned from a long and frustrating day in the Whitehall corridors of power, and was far from pleased to learn that, in his absence, the Robot had been found, and lost again; the Doctor had been knocked cold; and Miss Smith had gone off on a wild, dangerous and unauthorised mission with the one and only independent witness !

'Did you get permission to raid the Thinktank, sir?' asked Benton, hoping to divert the Brigadier's attention.

'No, Mr. Benton, I did not. Whitehall refuse to consider any such move without what they term "substantial and convincing evidence".'

The door opened and the Doctor came in, yawning and stretching. He perched himself on the Brigadier's desk and said, 'Now see here, Brigadier, you've got to tell me what was in that vault at that house. I know the *sort* of thing it was—the key to some kind of ultimate threat. But I need to know exactly.'

The Brigadier brooded for a moment and then nodded. 'Mr. Benton, Doctor,' he said, 'I am the only member of this organisation with a sufficiently high security clearance to be in possession of that information. I am releasing it to you solely because of the present emergency. It is to be divulged to no one.'

Benton nodded solemnly, somewhat overawed.

The Doctor said, 'Do get on with it, old chap.'

Some time ago, the Brigadier told them, the European

powers had finalised an amazing scheme to preserve peace. They had all agreed to reveal the locations and computer firing codes of their hidden atomic missile sites to representatives of a chosen country. The idea was that, in the event of any threat of war, the country chosen could threaten to release *all* the information, thus causing a military stalemate.

'Naturally enough,' the Brigadier went on, 'the only country that could be trusted with such a role was Great Britain.'

'Naturally,' said the Doctor solemnly. 'I mean, the rest were all foreigners.'

Ignoring the interruption, the Brigadier continued. 'The Destructor Codes were in the Minister's safe. They were all stolen when he was killed.'

Benton shook his head, trying to take it all in. 'So what can they do with this info now they've got it?'

It was the Doctor who answered the question. 'Assuming, as we must, that they've got accomplices planted in the right places, they could set off every atomic missile in Europe. They could start a world war, a nuclear holocaust that would turn this little planet of yours into a radioactive cinder hanging in space.'.

There followed a moment's silence. Benton, still puzzled asked, 'So why would they want to do that? I mean, they'd only go up with the rest of us!'

The Doctor said, 'I don't suppose they *want* to do it. But they might very well *threaten* to do it.'

Benton nodded. 'I get it now, Doctor. They'll try and blackmail the world. Do things our way or we'll light the blue touch paper?'

The Brigadier sighed. 'We might have been able to use Professor Kettlewell's evidence to convince the Government.' He glared reproachfully at Benton. 'If it wasn't for the fact that Miss Smith seems to have dragged him off on some wild goose chase.'

The Doctor sprang to his feet. 'Kettlewell!' he said, appalled. 'You let her go off somewhere with Kettlewell? Don't you realise—he's the one behind the whole thing!'

# 8

## In the Hands of the Enemy

Crammed into a space between the wall and a huge metal filing cabinet, Sarah crouched and listened as the speeches droned on. Folding chairs had been set up in rows across the hall to accommodate the audience. At the far end from Sarah's hiding place, a table and chairs for the speakers had been set up on the little stage. Beside her on the floor an ultra-sensitive tape-recorder whirled away, and although her angle of vision was limited she was doing her best to photograph the committee and audience with her miniature camera. However, the speeches so far had been as innocent as they were boring. Sarah thought that if things didn't warm up soon, she might just as well go home.

Suddenly a familiar figure came through the curtains at the back of the little stage. Miss Winters! And Jellicoe was tagging along behind her. Miss Winters began her speech and, to Sarah's surprise, she turned out to be a real rabble-rouser. She spoke of the years of scorn and neglect they had all endured, and of the future in which they, the élite, would rule—as was their right. The audience in the little hall applauded thunderously, and

Sarah saw that the everyday faces around her were afire with terrifying fanaticism. Miss Winters held up her hand for silence. 'We owe much of our success to one man, the man whose scientific genius has put real power within our grasp—Professor Jeremiah Kettlewell!' Kettlewell strode proudly on to the stage, modestly acknowledging the cheers of his audience.

Miss Winters raised her hand again. 'The Professor brings with him the symbol of our movement, the being whose intelligence, power and purity make it a fitting emblem for our scientific and rational new order!'

Sarah watched in amazement as the giant metal form of the Robot stalked on to the platform and stood looking down at the awe-stricken audience. She leaned forward and rapidly began to take as many photographs as she could: Kettlewell, Miss Winters, Jellicoe *and* the Robot. A nice little group for the Brigadier's family album.

Meanwhile, a disturbance was taking place at the door. The bouncer was arguing with an odd-looking character in a long scarf and a floppy wide-brimmed hat. The Doctor, disregarding the Brigadier's protests, had insisted on acting as a one man advance guard. He had adamantly refused to wait until a proper armed party could be organised.

'Look mate,' said the exasperated bouncer, 'I keep telling you: no membership card, no go in, right?'

The Doctor searched through his pockets, hopefully offering various other credentials. He pulled out an ornate scroll. 'Freedom of the City of Skaro . . . no . . . Pilot's licence for the Mars-venus rocket run . . . no. How about this: honorary member of the Alpha Centauri table tennis club? Very tricky opponents those chaps. Six arms, six bats you see. Really keep you on your toes . . .' The bouncer looked threatening and the Doctor said, 'You don't want to be bothered with all this non-

78

sense, do you? Tell you what, I'll just pop inside . . .'

The Doctor tried to slip past the table, but the bouncer had been expecting this move. His big hands reached out to grasp the Doctor in the celebrated stranglehold that had served him so well during his days as a wrestler. Unfortunately the Doctor refused to be held. He slipped to one side and the bouncer's hands gripped empty air. Worse still, one of the Doctor's long legs somehow got tangled round the bouncer's ankle, and he tripped over his chair and fell on top of the table, which collapsed beneath him.

The Doctor surveyed the wreckage. 'Why don't you just sit there and get some rest?' he suggested kindly. 'I'll go and get you some help.'

Slipping into the lobby, the Doctor looked through the double doors into the crowded hall. He could see rows of backs of heads, and there on the little stage Miss Winters, Jellicoe, Kettlewell and the Robot! Deciding that this was where things were happening, the Doctor hurried down the corridor that led to the back-stage area.

Sarah's mind was full of questions throughout Miss Winters' speech. If Kettlewell was part of the conspiracy, why had he brought her here? Why hadn't she been discovered? She considered making a dash for it, but her filing cabinet stood in the middle of one wall, and she'd never reach the door without being caught.

Miss Winters was still ranting away on the stage . . . 'Naturally, we have not achieved all this without opposition. There have been those who have sought to spy on us, to betray our cause to the so-called authorities.'

With a feeling of dread, Sarah began to realise why she had been left so long in her hiding place. Her capture was to be stage-managed to provide a spectacle—encouragement for the faithful! She was not surprised when Miss Winters came to the climax of her speech.

'But they will not succeed. We shall seek out and destroy all those who try to oppose us!'

The Robot began to stalk through the audience towards Sarah's hiding place. It lifted the big filing cabinet to one side, revealing Sarah crouched with her tape-recorder and camera. Miss Winters came down from the platform, Jellicoe and Kettlewell following her.

She pointed at Sarah with a deliberately dramatic gesture. 'She's a spy—and we know how to deal with spies, don't we?'

An ugly growl rose from the crowd, and they began to surge forward. Jellicoe muttered, 'Stop them—you've got them so worked up they'll tear her to pieces.' Miss Winters said nothing. She watched with evident enjoyment as the crowd closed in on Sarah. Her tape-recorder and camera were smashed. Sarah, struggling wildly, was grabbed.

Suddenly a strange voice rang out. 'Good evening, ladies and gentlemen.'

Everyone turned. A tall man in a long scarf and floppy hat was occupying the centre of the stage—like an old-fashioned, eccentric comedian. 'Now then,' he said cheerfully, 'what can I do to entertain you until my good friend the Brigadier arrives with his merry men? A comic song? A little tap dancing?' The Doctor managed to perform quite a creditable little jig. His manner and appearance were so irresistibly comic that several of the audience began to laugh. Someone actually started clapping. The Doctor seemed much encouraged. 'Thank you sir, thank you! Now then, what about a few card tricks?' He produced a pack of cards and sprayed them up in the air in a kind of fountain, catching them neatly and shuffling them back into the pack.

Miss Winters was furious. The carefully built-up atmosphere had been completely destroyed by this mountebank! He seemed perfectly capable of keeping these fools happy until the Brigadier arrived to lock them all up. At that moment, the massive, battered figure of the bouncer staggered through the double doors. He had just managed to disentangle himself from the shattered table. 'Some bloke,' he was muttering thickly, 'some bloke come in and—where is he?'

Miss Winters pointed towards the stage. 'There he is. Get him.'

As the bouncer shouldered his way through the crowd, the Doctor was saying, 'Now, for my next trick, I shall require the assistance of a sporting gentleman from the audience!' The bouncer started clambering on the stage and the Doctor said, 'You, sir? How very kind! Let me assist you!' The Doctor held out a helping hand, and the bouncer automatically took it. The Doctor heaved, twisted, and somehow the bouncer found himself flying through the air.

He crashed in to the wall head first and lost all further interest in the Doctor.

Miss Winters was beside herself with rage. 'That man is another spy. He's endangering us all. Get him, you fools.'

The younger and more active members of the SRS began to climb on to the stage. A brief free-for-all followed. The Doctor disappeared beneath a heaving pile of arms and legs. Minutes later, battered but still cheerful, he was pulled from the bottom of the pile and dragged towards Miss Winters. Ignoring her, he said, 'Hullo, Sarah!' The Doctor turned to the little figure of Kettlewell who was lurking in the background. 'Tell me one thing, Professor,' he asked. 'Why?'

Sarah could see that Kettlewell found it difficult to meet the Doctor's eye. He shuffled his feet and stared at the floor. 'Because, Doctor, I have been trying to *persuade* people to stop polluting this planet for years.

Now, with the help of my friends here, I shall be able to *make* them stop!'

The Doctor sighed. 'I thought it must be something like that. You're forgetting something, old chap. In morals or in science, the end *never* justifies the means.'

Kettlewell turned to Miss Winters. 'What are you going to do with him?'

'Kill him, of course. He's far too dangerous to us.'

Kettlewell was obviously appalled. 'Couldn't we just lock him up, until it's all over?'

'And risk his escape? It's too late to be squeamish now.'

The Doctor looked at Kettlewell almost sympathetically. 'You see what I mean?'

It was obvious that Kettlewell did. Sarah could tell by the expression on the little man's face that the ruthlessness of his associates was having a shattering effect. Miss Winters turned to the men holding the Doctor and Sarah. 'Take them down to the cellars.'

They began struggling desperately, but their opponents were too many. Slowly they were dragged towards the door . . .

A shot rang out in the little hall. Another newcomer had taken the stage. The Brigadier, holding a smoking revolver in his hand and aided by Benton and a contingent of UNIT troops, began to address the mob below.

'Stay where you are! My men have this place completely surrounded.'

Immediate pandemonium followed. The panic-stricken SRS members totally ignored the Brigadier's order and ran frantically in all directions. UNIT troops flooded into the hall to try and restrain them, and the place became packed with a milling crowd of struggling bodies. The troops were handicapped by the fact that the Brigadier, despite his warning shot, had no intention of opening fire on unarmed civilians, and had given orders that no one was to shoot unless the enemy shot first.

The Doctor and Sarah were swept apart by the struggling crowds. The Doctor managed to break free from the men holding him, but the press of struggling bodies prevented him reaching Sarah. She was firmly grabbed by Jellicoe, who twisted her arm behind her. All this time, the Robot stood motionless. No one had ordered it to do anything else.

Miss Winters grabbed Kettlewell by the shoulders, and shoved him savagely towards the Robot. 'Make that thing get us out of here. We've got to escape to the car park.'

In a trembling voice, Kettlewell said, 'Activate! We must leave now. You will protect us.'

Effortlessly, the Robot began to force a path through the tightly packed mass, pushing the crowd aside as a boat cuts through water. Kettlewell and Miss Winters followed close behind. Jellicoe brought up the rear, backing away after them with Sarah held before him as a shield.

The Doctor saw what was happening and tried desperately to fight his way through the crowd to Sarah. He had almost reached her when the metal hand of the Robot gripped his arm, lifted him off his feet and flung him away into the crowd. The Doctor went down, scattering bodies like skittles, and the fleeing mob trampled over him.

From the stage the Brigadier watched helplessly as the Robot cleared a path towards the door. He raised his revolver, but dared not fire for fear of hitting Sarah. The little group disappeared through the rear door and vanished from sight.

Sarah fought fiercely, but Jellicoe was stronger than he looked, and he held her in a savage arm lock. Still struggling, she was dragged out of the hall, across the car park, and hurled into the back of the horse-box she had noticed earlier. Kettlewell, Miss Winters, and, finally, the Robot followed her. Jellicoe slammed the doors and ran round to the drivers cab. The horse-box roared away at top speed. Crashing through the barrier that UNIT troops had set up across the entrance, it sped off down the road. Benton, who had struggled out of the hall after the group, sprang into a Land-Rover and shot off in pursuit.

Inside the hall, order was gradually being restored. One by one the fleeing SRS members were collared, restrained and shepherded into UNIT lorries; until at last the Doctor and the Brigadier had the place almost to themselves.

The Doctor, a little tattered but otherwise unhurt, sat on the edge of the stage, swinging his legs and surveying the wreckage. Broken folding chairs were scattered about the room, and brawny soldiers were more or less carrying out the last struggling SRS members.

'It had to be Kettlewell, of course,' the Doctor was saying. 'Only he could have reprogrammed the Robot to overcome its Prime Directive—and luckily even he wasn't completely successful.'

The Brigadier snorted. 'Then all that business about being knocked out and shut in a cupboard . . .'

'They faked it all between them. When the ambush didn't work, Kettlewell still had a chance to gain your confidence.'

'If you suspected all this, Doctor, why didn't you tell us?'

'Well, I didn't get much chance, did I? I wasn't completely sure until Kettlewell set up that ambush. And by the time I'd got over that bang on the head, you'd let Sarah go off with him.'

'I did no such thing, Doctor, as you very well know—'

He broke off as Benton came in, carrying a UNIT

walkie-talkie set. 'I'm afraid I lost them, sir. That horse-box streaked away from me. Engine must have been specially souped up!'

The Brigadier looked as though he was about to explode. Hurriedly Benton went on, 'Call for you, sir, linked in from UNIT H.Q. It's Doctor Sullivan.'

Harry Sullivan was enjoying himself at Thinktank. He had been thoroughly officious and obnoxious, and had made them turn out all the records for his inspection. He had criticised their filing system, and had even carried out one or two genuine medical examinations—just to make things look convincing. Towards the end of the day, he had tucked himself away in his little cubbyhole, claiming that his record-checking wasn't quite complete.

When everything was quiet, he'd crept cautiously out, and started prowling round the corridors of Thinktank, looking for evidence—of what he didn't quite know. A number of the labs seemed to be empty; others looked prepared to work all night. Finally he had made his way to Miss Winters' office and begun searching it. Cheerfully breaking open a number of locked filing cabinets, he had uncovered some rather interesting correspondence with other scientific institutions all over the world—much of it in code. Harry piled everything that looked suspicious into his doctor's bag, intending to hand it over to the Brigadier.

As he was nearing the end of his search, he heard the sound of activity from the courtyard below. Peering through the window, he saw a horse-box speed through the main gates and draw up at the front entrance. Jellicoe jumped out of the front, and let Miss Winters out of the back. Both ran into the building. A moment later a security guard ran out of the building, jumped into the front of the horse-box and drove it away. Bells began to ring, security men and laboratory workers ran out to their cars and drove away after the van.

Harry thought for a moment, picked up the phone, and dialled the number for UNIT H.Q. After an agonising delay while the call was linked to the radio network, he found himself talking to the Brigadier. Hurriedly, Harry reported his discoveries, and told the Brigadier of the new developments. 'They seem to be pulling out, sir. I get the feeling the whole place is being evacuated. Some kind of prearranged plan'.

'Sullivan, this is urgent. Have you *any* idea where they're going?' Harry could hear the tension in the Brigadier's voice.

'Afraid not, sir . . . hang on a moment. While I was snooping about earlier, I heard a couple of chaps saying it would soon be time to take to the Bunker. Seemed to be some kind of joke . . .'

Harry was so absorbed in his conversation that he didn't see the security guard appear in the office doorway. The man moved silently towards him, rubber-soled shoes making no sound on the office floor. At the last moment Harry heard his breathing and whirled round— but it was too late. A truncheon crashed down, Harry felt a moment's agonising pain, and everything went black.

# 9

## The Battle at the Bunker

The Brigadier shook the radio irritably. 'Line's gone dead. Sullivan must have got cut off.'

'Or found out.' said the Doctor. 'Still, at least we know

where to start looking. Let's go and visit the Thinktank, Brigadier!'

The Brigadier began rapping out orders and in an amazingly short time a little convoy of vehicles was on its way towards Thinktank. In front was the Brigadier in his Land-Rover, the Doctor beside him. Behind followed lorry loads of UNIT troops.

As they drove up to Thinktank's main gates, they were astonished to see them standing open and unguarded. The front door of the main building was open, too. All the lights were blazing, but there was no other sign of life. As they ran up the steps and into the building, the Doctor thought of the *Marie Celeste*. The offices and the laboratories were deserted. The Brigadier ordered a thorough search of the building and he and the Doctor made their way to the Director's office. It too was open and empty. The filing cabinets had also been cleaned out.

The Brigadier looked round. 'Well, Doctor, now what?'

The Doctor perched on Miss Winters' desk and twirled his long scarf like a cowboy's lassoo. 'I think the answer lies in something Mr. Benton said not long ago.'

Benton joined them in the office in time to hear this. 'Far as we can see, sir, the place is completely empty,' he reported. 'Excuse me, Doctor, did you say something *I* said?'

The Doctor nodded. 'Something about the Thinktank people going up with the rest of us if they started a nuclear war. If they're prepared to do more than just bluff—and I think they are—you'd think they'd have some kind of refuge prepared. There can't be *that* many possibilities . . .'

The Brigadier gave a sudden strangled yelp. 'That's it! Why the blazes didn't I think of that earlier! Mr.

Benton, Doctor, come with me!' He tore out of the room, with Benton and the Doctor hard on his tail.

'Excuse me, sir,' panted Benton as they hared down the Thinktank corridors. 'Where exactly are we off to?'

'To the Bunker, Mr. Benton,' said the Brigadier over his shoulder.

'So I assume,' added the Doctor rather crossly. 'Would you be good enough to tell us where it is?'

The Brigadier beamed. 'Believe it or not, Doctor, it's literally at the bottom of the garden.'

Soon the UNIT convoy was on its way again, speeding through the extensive park-like grounds that surrounded Thinktank. The Brigadier drove to a stretch of rough, wooded land at the far end of the grounds. He stood up in the Land-Rover, and pointed with his swagger stick. 'There, Doctor, is the Bunker.' He indicated a massive concrete building, nestling in a tree-surrounded hollow just ahead of them. It was built in the shape of a squared-off letter U, its two long wings linked by one short one which was crowned with a tower. A concrete path led between the two arms of the U to a massive metal door which formed the only break in the concrete façade.

'An experimental atomic bomb shelter,' said the Brigadier triumphantly. 'Built by the Thinktank people themselves. Designed to allow a small community to survive almost indefinitely. Own power, food supplies, water, air-purifying equipment. Completely self-contained! I remember reading a report about it. Government tried to cancel the project since the worst of the Cold War days seem to be over. But the Thinktank people managed to push it through. I never did understand why they were so keen . . .' The Brigadier's voice tailed off, as he realised what he was saying. 'They had it all planned, right from the beginning!'

The Doctor nodded. 'If their bluff *is* called, they start

their atomic war, stay down there safe and sound, and emerge to rule the survivors—if any.'

'We'll see about that,' said the Brigadier. 'Mr. Benton, demolition party, please. We'll winkle our friends out of their shell!'

The Doctor, the Brigadier, Benton and UNIT soldiers, loaded down with the latest in high-powered plastic explosives, made their way cautiously along the concrete path. As they came near the door, the two long arms of the U-shaped building seemed to close in on them menacingly. The Doctor looked round warily. He appeared almost to be sniffing the air. His keen eyes constantly swept the featureless concrete walls, alert for any change. Suddenly he yelled, 'Look out! *Down*, all of you!' The Doctor stretched out his long arms and threw himself backwards, sweeping everyone behind him off the path. A sudden chattering of machine-gun fire filled the air, as a murderously efficient cross-fire swept the entire area.

Hurriedly the little party scrambled back to the safety of the Land-Rover.

The Brigadier was furious. 'Well of all the ruddy cheek! They've actually got troops here!'

The Doctor shook his head. 'I don't think so. Automated gun nests, I fancy. Probably activated by body heat as you approach.'

The radio in the Land-Rover suddenly began to crackle. Benton picked it up and fiddled with it. 'I think someone's trying to get through on our frequency, sir.'

The voice of Miss Winters came from the set, distorted by atmospherics but perfectly recognisable. 'Brigadier, I am speaking to you from the Bunker. Can you hear me?'

The Brigadier snatched the radio. 'I hear you, Madam. You will kindly come out and surrender yourself immediately.'

Even over the radio, the self-satisfaction in the cold voice was unmistakable. 'I shall do no such thing, Brigadier. This place is impregnable, as you very well know. You have already had a taste of our automatic defence system.'

'You will come out, or you will be blown out,' said the Brigadier. 'Surrender now and you won't be hurt. Resist, and you will take the consequences.'

The unseen speaker seemed to pause a little, as if disconcerted by this prompt reply. Then the voice came again. 'You forget, Brigadier. We hold two of your friends as hostages. Doctor Sullivan and Miss Smith are our prisoners.'

The Brigadier cast a brief, agonised glance at the Doctor. The tone of his reply, however, was as even as before. 'That will not deter me from my duty. I repeat, surrender now or we shall attack.'

Miss Winters' voice filled with cold fury. 'You'll never reach those doors alive, Brigadier. If you did, you'd never get through them. I suggest you contact your superiors. By now the Government will have received our demands. Unless they are agreed to in full, we shall use the Destructor Codes. *You* have one hour in which to surrender.'

The set went dead. The Brigadier tossed it back in the Land-Rover. 'That woman's absolutely raving mad!'

The Doctor sighed. 'You're probably right. But she means what she says.'

'So do I, Doctor. Mr. Benton, bring up the bazooka and some grenades. We'll start by knocking out those machine-gun nests.'

Deep inside the Bunker, the circular control room was buzzing with activity. It held a radio-communications set-up, a monitor screen on which automatic cameras showed the approach to the main doors, and the control system for the Bunker. A computer terminal with its own complex numerical keyboard occupied the rest of the room. Above this keyboard a large digital count-down clock was standing motionless at the number 600. Six hundred seconds—which equals ten minutes.

Miss Winters, Jellicoe and Kettlewell were gazing at the monitor. It showed the path which stretched away from the main doors, and at the end of it the Brigadier's little group of vehicles. They could even pick out the Brigadier and the Doctor standing by the leading Land-Rover.

Jellicoe said nervously, 'Do you think they'd go ahead with the attack?'

Miss Winter's voice was calm. 'I'm sure of it. The Brigadier's an obstinate man.' From a briefcase by her side she produced a book. Bound in black leather, it was approximately the size of a school exercise book. The words DESTRUCTOR CODES were stamped on the cover in gold letters. She tossed the book to Kettlewell, who caught it awkwardly. 'You'd better begin familiarising yourself with this, Professor Kettlewell. I think we're going to have to fire the missiles.'

Not far away, Harry Sullivan and Sarah Jane sat side by side, bound hand and foot to identical wooden chairs. Behind them stood the Robot. The two prisoners had finished comparing notes about their respective adventures, and now sat in despondent silence. The little store-room in which they were held was lined with row upon row of shelves, packed with every imaginable variety of tinned and powdered foods. Harry nodded towards them. 'Well at least we won't go hungry.'

'Nor will the people keeping us here,' said Sarah. 'What do you think they're going to do with us?'

Harry shruggled. 'We're hostages, I imagine. Though it won't do them any good.'

'What do you mean?'

'Well, if they do try to use us as a lever, the Brig won't listen. I mean, he can't, can he?'

'No,' said Sarah slowly. 'I suppose he can't.'

Harry craned his head to peer over his shoulder. The Robot was just standing there, motionless, and apparently lifeless. Harry started to struggle with his bonds, gently at first, and then more vigorously. Sarah saw what he was doing, and she too began trying to free herself.

Suddenly an enormous metal hand clamped down on Harry's shoulder. A booming voice said, 'DO NOT MOVE. IF YOU ATTEMPT TO ESCAPE I MUST DESTROY YOU.'

They both sat rigid.


Outside the Bunker, the job of knocking out the automated machine-gun nests was almost over. It had been a slow and dangerous business. First a soldier had to move close enough to the door for the Bunker's sensor devices to detect his body heat and activate the machine-guns. Then he had to jump back quickly enough to save himself from getting killed. Already two soldiers had been wounded by cutting it too fine. Other soldiers waited with bazookas and grenades, and watched for the opening of the machine-gun ports. To knock them out, it was necessary to score a direct hit on each gun before the protective ports could close again. The Doctor noticed that for all the rain of explosives that had poured onto it, the building was quite unscarred. It was obviously made of no ordinary concrete.

One by one the machine-gun defences were silenced. At last, only a solitary gun chattered out when the soldier dodged near. It was awkwardly placed and Benton and the others blazed away at it in vain.

The Doctor watched from the Land-Rover, occasionally

sticking his fingers in his ears when the noise became un-
bearable. The Brigadier had spent most of the time on
the RT, calling up reinforcements, and talking on a
direct radio link to Downing Street.

The Brigadier put down his radio. 'Well, it's just as
we expected, Doctor. Thinktank have made a number
of completely unacceptable demands. To agree would
mean surrendering the country into their hands. The
Cabinet is unanimous. No surrender, and no compromise.
We're to knock them out. We can have any help we need.
I've already ordered—'

'My dear Brigadier,' interrupted the Doctor testily,
'nothing your Government can give us is likely to be of
the slightest help. Up to and including an atomic bomb!
More to the point, are they taking steps to prevent those
lunatics in there from firing all the missiles in Europe?'

'They're doing all they can, Doctor. But frankly, it
doesn't seem to be much. We can't even cut off their
power. They've got their own nuclear generator in there!'

'Surely the missile systems have a fail-safe mechanism?'

The Brigadier nodded grimly. 'It's being operated
now. Unfortunately, it happens to be extremely complex to set up. If Thinktank's claims are true, they can
fire the majority of the missiles in just ten minutes—long
before the fail-safe can take effect.'

The Doctor shook his head despairingly. 'Then at
least they can tell the world what's happening. Tell them
that if the missiles do start falling it won't be an act of
war, but a plot by a small group of criminals.'

'That's being done too, Doctor. But what are our
chances of being believed? If just one missile falls on
Russia or China—or one of the new African states that
have just got atomic power . . .' The Brigadier shuddered.
'They'll blast away with everything they've got!'

The Doctor leaned wearily against the Land-Rover. 'If

this ferocious little species of yours didn't insist on piling up these terrible weapons . . .'

'That doesn't help us at the moment,' snapped the Brigadier, who had no intention of listening to a lecture on the folly of mankind. 'The hour's nearly up—and it's up to us to get in there and stop that countdown before it starts.'

The last machine gun fell silent, and Benton came running up and saluted. 'That's the lot, sir. I scored a direct hit with a grenade !'

'And about time, too. Right men, forward !' As the Brigadier set off, the Doctor stretched out a long arm and tapped his shoulder. 'Just a moment, there's a good chap !'

The Doctor produced his sonic screwdriver—a futuristic, multipurpose torch-like device. He made a few adjustments, then walked cautiously down the concrete path, 'sweeping' the device to and fro before him—rather like a water-diviner. He reached the point where the machine guns had opened up before. Silence. The Brigadier smiled in satisfaction. The Doctor moved on, still waving the sonic screwdriver. Suddenly, the path immediately ahead of him exploded. Smoke and flames billowed up from the ground. Face blackened and eyebrows singed, the Doctor moved on. As he swept the area before and around him with the sonic screwdriver, mine after mine began to explode. When the Doctor stopped, the air was full of smoke and the ground was churned up like a battlefield after days of shelling. The Doctor grinned, teeth white in his smoke-blackened face, and waved the Brigadier and his men forward. 'Come along, then !'

Cautiously they moved to join him as he stood looking up at the massive metal door. 'Your last obstacle, Brigadier.'

The Brigadier examined the huge door with an air of grim determination. 'Super reinforced steel set in super reinforced concrete. Still, we can but try! Explosives please, Mr. Benton!'

The Doctor winced. 'Oh no! Haven't we had enough bangs and flashes for the moment? Hang on.' He made a series of complex adjustments to his sonic screwdriver.

The Brigadier looked on impatiently. 'Time's nearly up, Doctor. What are you going to do, pick the lock with that thing?'

'Better than that. I'll cut it out for you.'

The end of the sonic screwdriver began to glow red, and the Doctor started inscribing a circle round the lock area. 'Works like a miniature sonic lance,' he proudly instructed.

The Brigadier said, 'You're wasting your time, Doctor. Even the latest, full-size thermic lance couldn't . . .' He fell silent, his mouth agape in amazement. A fiery red circle was appearing in the door, and the metal was melting away like butter!

'Takes a minute or two,' said the Doctor airily. 'But at least it's *quiet* !'

Inside the Bunker the little group of conspirators were huddled together in the control room. Jellicoe was studying the dials on the control panel before him. 'Machine guns knocked out, mines de-activated. What about your precious defence system now?'

'There's still the door,' said Miss Winters confidently. 'Made from the toughest alloy in the world. Nothing can—'

A panic-stricken cry from Kettlewell interrupted her. 'They're cutting through. Look—it's the Doctor! He's cutting through your precious door like cheese!'

He indicated the monitor screen which showed a close-up of the Doctor happily at work on the door. The glowing circle was now almost complete.

Miss Winters shoved Kettlewell towards the computer terminal. 'Use the Destructor Codes, Professor. We'll have to *show* them we're not bluffing.'

'It's a complex business,' said Kettlewell distractedly. 'If they're going to break through any minute, it isn't even worth starting the pre-count-down sequence . . .'

Miss Winters shoved him in to the chair. 'Start the sequence, Professor. We'll use your metal friend to buy us a little time.'

She turned and strode from the room, Jellicoe following. Left alone, Kettlewell sat staring at the computer keyboard. Slowly he opened the black leather book and started punching the controls.

Outside the Bunker the Doctor felt a sudden vibration through the door. He leaped to his feet. 'Back everybody. Something's happening.'

As they backed away they saw a fine line appear in the centre of the metal door. It widened slowly into a gap. 'Look, sir,' said Benton. 'They're opening up!'

Slowly, very slowly, the gap widened. The Brigadier said hopefully, 'Maybe they've come to their senses, decided to surrender.'

The Doctor looked sceptical. 'Maybe. Somehow I doubt it, though. Better pull further back until we're sure what's happening.'

The little group backed away almost to the end of the path. They waited as the doors slid back to their full extent. At first they revealed only a patch of blackness.

Then a huge metal shape stepped out. In one hand it held a strange-looking gun—a sort of huge, futuristic-looking rifle. It swung the gun up and fired with amazing speed. The nearest soldier glowed red and vanished in a blaze of incredible heat. The Doctor yelled, 'Get your men back, Brigadier, or they'll all be killed!'

The Brigadier shouted, 'You heard the Doctor. Pull back on the double!'

As the soldiers ran for the shelter of the trees, a booming voice rang in their ears. 'YOU ARE ENEMIES OF HUMANITY. GO! GO NOW OR I SHALL DESTROY YOU ALL!'

The Bunker doors slowly closed again. Before them, Disintegrator Gun at the ready, the Robot stood waiting, defying them to attack!

## 10

## The Countdown Begins

From their shelter beneath the trees, the Doctor and the Brigadier looked back at the Robot. The Doctor threw his wide-brimmed hat down in frustration. 'We were so nearly through! Another few minutes...'

A sudden grinding and clanking came from behind them. The Brigadier swung round, his face lighting up. 'Don't worry, Doctor. I've got something to deal with it now!'

The Doctor saw a tank lumbering towards them. The Brigadier ran up to it, had a quick word with the rather astonished tank commander, and pointed towards the Robot.

The commander nodded confidently and popped back inside his tank. Slowly the tank rolled across the churned-up path towards the Bunker doors, stopping about fifty feet from the Robot. For a long moment, the two metal monsters confronted one another. The big gun on the tank's main turret swivelled round to cover the Robot. The Disintegrator Gun in the Robot's hands came up.

Both fired together. The tank glowed red, then exploded into nothingness.

Inside the Bunker, Miss Winters watched the scene on her monitor. She smiled, quite unmoved by the destruction of the tank and the deaths of its crew. She turned to Kettlewell, who had been looking in horror at the screen. 'That seems to be very satisfactory. How are you getting on, Professor?'

Kettlewell brought his attention back to the computer terminal. 'I've completed the preliminary link-ups.'

'Excellent! I suggest you begin the countdown.'

Kettlewell looked appalled. 'Surely you don't intend to *use* the Destructor Codes?'

'They've left us no alternative.'

'But we *can't*. It'll start a nuclear war.'

Miss Winters raised her eyebrows. 'You want a better world, don't you? We shan't achieve it without some sacrifices.' Her voice hardened. 'Start the countdown, Professor.'

Reluctantly Kettlewell pressed a series of controls. The digital clock above his head clicked into life. The numbers began to count down. 599, 598, 597 . . . They seemed to flicker across the screen at tremendous speed. With a sense of rising horror, Kettlewell thought he had never realised how short a second really was . . . 590, 589, 587. Busily the numbers flickered on, ticking away the life of the planet in measured seconds . . .


Freed from the supervision of the Robot, Harry and Sarah were both struggling desperately with their bonds. They had worked their chairs round back to back so that

Sarah's fingers could reach the knots on Harry's wrists. 'How are you doing?' he asked.

Sarah's fingers were almost numb, but she didn't complain. 'It's coming,' she said. 'I think it's coming.'

They heard footsteps, and then Miss Winters' voice. 'We must make a full check of the supply situation. We need to know exactly how long we can hold out.'

At frantic speed Sarah and Harry wriggled the chairs back to their former positions. Moments later Jellicoe and Miss Winters appeared in the doorway.

Jellicoe indicated the prisoners. 'What about these two?'

Miss Winters said coolly, 'They're no use to us as hostages, and we can't afford to feed useless mouths. They'll have to be disposed of.'

Jellicoe took a step towards them, almost eagerly. It was obvious that his new-found position of power had brought out a streak of sadism. 'Now?' he asked.

'Later. We'll start the check in the end storage bay.' Miss Winters led Jellicoe away.

'That was a near one,' muttered Harry. 'We'd better get a move on.'

They wriggled their chairs back to back again and Sarah set to work on Harry's knots with renewed urgency. Suddenly, one of the tangled loops of cord came free. Harry said, 'All right, wait a minute.' He flexed the muscles of his arms and strained at it with all his strength. Ignoring the pain of the rope cutting into his wrists, he managed to wrench one hand free, the wrist slippery with blood. With a triumphant grin he set about freeing his other wrist.

Outside, the Brigadier was holding a council of war. He nodded towards the Robot, which still continued its

99

solitary guard. 'This Disintegrator Gun, Doctor. What's its range and power?'

'Power—more or less unlimited. Range—well, it could drill a hole in the surface of the moon. The ingenuity of your species in devising weapons of destruction . . .'

'All right, all right, Doctor.' The Brigadier did not wish to be reminded that he was being almost literally hoist with humanity's own petard. *He* hadn't invented the wretched gun. Or the Robot either, come to that.

'So it can knock out anything we send against it?'

'I'm afraid so.' The Doctor got to his feet. 'Well, no use standing here, is it? Brigadier, you must prepare your men for a full-scale attack on the Robot. Use everything you've got. They won't be able to harm it, but with any luck they'll draw it away from those doors. I'll try to slip round behind it, and finish cutting through.'

Slowly the Brigadier rose. The plan was suicidal. There was almost no chance that the troops would be able to distract the Robot long enough to enable the Doctor to succeed. Most likely, they would all be blasted into nothingness. It was, however, obvious that the Doctor was quite aware of the risks.

'There's nothing else we *can* do,' said the Doctor gently. 'And we've got to try, haven't we?'

The Brigadier nodded. 'Yes, Doctor, we have to try.' Quickly he turned away and went to brief his men.

The Doctor stood looking at the Robot for a moment. It was ironical, he thought, that his new life was almost certainly going to be over before it had properly begun. He sighed. So much to see, so much to do. A universe to explore . . .

The Brigadier's men began to form up. The Doctor produced his sonic screwdriver and gave it a final check.

300, 299, 298 . . . Less than five minutes to go. In the Bunker, Kettlewell suddenly knew that he *could not* allow the countdown to go on. The Doctor's words seemed to echo inside his head. 'The end *never* justifies the means . . .' However worthy his motives, he was going to be responsible for the deaths of thousands, millions of people. 'I can't do it,' he sobbed. 'I won't.' He stabbed at the keyboard . . . 289, 288— The numbers stopped moving.

A voice spoke behind him. 'Why has the countdown stopped?'

Jellicoe stood in the doorway of the control room. He had been unable to resist watching the actual moment when the first missile would be fired. Kettlewell faced him bravely. 'It's been stopped because I'm not going throught with it.'

Jellicoe produced a revolver. 'Resume the countdown, Professor. Or I'll kill you and finish it myself.' He raised the revolver. Kettlcwell realised the man was unbalanced. He would be glad of an excuse to carry out his threat. Kettlewell's courage crumbled, and he returned to the keyboard. 287, 286, 285 . . . The countdown resumed its remorseless progress. Jellicoe smiled. A little over four and a half minutes and—

Someone tapped him on the shoulder. Jellicoe swung round to face Harry Sullivan, Sarah at his shoulder. It was the last thing he saw for some time. As he raised his revolver, a large fist exploded under his jaw. Harry had floored him with a classic upper-cut.

Harry stepped aside to let Jellicoe fall, rubbing his knuckles with quiet satisfaction.

Sarah was shaking Kettlewell by the shoulder. The little man seemed dazed. 'Professor Kettlewell,' she said urgently, 'can you reverse that countdown?'

He looked at her wild-eyed. 'It would take too long to

switch off completely. I can punch in a "hold" signal. I did it a moment ago, only Jellicoe made me . . .'

'Never mind that now,' said Sarah impatiently. 'Just *stop* the thing.'

'Then open the main door,' added Harry, 'We've got to get out of here.'

Kettlewell's will-power seemed to have disappeared. Meekly he did as he was told. 256, 255, 254—. Once again, the countdown froze. Kettlewell activated the control to open the main door . . .

'Right,' said Harry. 'Let's get moving.' Almost dragging the little Professor between them, Sarah and Harry ran from the control room.


The Brigadier and his men had worked their way closer and closer to the Robot. The Brigadier took a deep breath. He was just about to give the order to attack when the Doctor tapped him on the shoulder. 'Look, the door's opening again. And there's Harry!' In the slowly widening gap between the doors they could see Harry peeping out, Sarah and Kettlewell close behind him.

Harry and the others looked out at the huge metal back of the Robot. The doors were opening quite silently, and it seemed unaware of them. When the gap was wide enough, they slipped out, first Harry, then Sarah. The little Professor hung back, as if uncertain that he really wanted to go. Sarah turned when she realised he wasn't following them. 'Come on, Professor,' she whispered. Low as her voice was, the Robot heard it. It swung round, levelling the Disintegrator Gun.

As the gun came up, Harry Sullivan grabbed Sarah and threw her by main force away from the danger area. With sudden courage, Kettlewell darted out and threw himself in front of the gun. The Robot had already fired. Kettlewell froze like a statue, and the red glow blasted him into nothingness.

Sarah and Harry stood quite still, both expecting to be the next targets. The UNIT party was too far away to be able to help them.

But the Robot was not concerned with them. It was reeling and staggering in a state of evident distress. The gun had fallen, forgotten, at its feet. With a note of agony in its voice it boomed, 'I HAVE KILLED THE ONE WHO CREATED ME!' Suddenly it collapsed. Its great weight lay motionless on the ground.

The Doctor tapped the Brigadier on the shoulder. 'Come on—this is our chance!' They sprinted at top speed towards Harry and Sarah, who were waiting by the open gate.

Her stores-check finished, Miss Winters entered the control room and found that her long-planned seizure of power had vanished like smoke in her hands. She took in the disaster at a glance: Jellicoe unconscious on the floor, the countdown arrested; and on the monitor screen UNIT troops were pouring into the Bunker past the apparently lifeless body of the Robot.

Miss Winters acted almost without thinking. If she couldn't have victory, she would have revenge. If she couldn't rule the world as she had planned, she would end it in flames. She sat at the keyboard and began punching controls. She could hear the sound of shooting outside the control room. Her hands moved faster over the keyboard. The digital clock came to life again. 253, 252, 251 . . . Miss Winters watched with quiet satisfaction.

The Brigadier and his men were facing spirited rear-guard action in the winding corridors of the Bunker. Some of the Thinktank staff had armed themselves and were resisting in a last burst of fanaticism. The air was loud with the sound of shots, and bullets ricocheted from the concrete walls.

Yards away from the battle area, and, shielded only by a turn of wall, Sarah, the Doctor and Harry were having a brief and joyful reunion. All three talked at once, breathlessly trying to explain to each other what had been happening.

Suddenly the gunfire stopped and Benton popped his head round the corner. 'That seems to be the last of 'em,' he said. Sarah and the others followed him down the smoke-filled corridors. She tried to avoid looking at the huddled figures strewn on the ground.

As they arrived at the control room, Sarah saw the Brigadier freeze. She pushed her way past Harry to the front of the group.

Miss Winters sat at the computer keyboard, a small automatic in her hand.

The Brigadier ordered: 'Get away from there!' He raised his revolver.

Miss Winters ignored him. 'You won't shoot, Brigadier,' she said confidently.

Sarah realised that she was right. The Brigadier was simply incapable of shooting a woman—even one who was armed and dangerous. Sarah caught sight of Jellicoe's revolver, which lay just by his outstretched hand. She shoved her way into the room, quickly scooped it up, and aimed it at Miss Winters. 'Maybe the Brigadier won't shoot, Miss Winters,' said Sarah. 'But *I* will. Now move away.'

For a moment the two women confronted each other. Miss Winters' eyes fell. She tossed her automatic on the floor and stood up. 'Why not? It's finished. The firing instructions are about to take effect.'

'Cancel them,' snapped the Brigadier.

Miss Winters indicated the digital clock. 'Too late. When the clock reaches zero the missiles will be fired. And it takes over ten minutes to send the cancel codes!'

They all looked at the digital clock. 59, 58, 57 . . . There was less than a minute to go.

## The Kidnapping of Sarah

The Brigadier's sense of chivalry finally deserted him. He grabbed Miss Winters by the shoulders and threw her across the room into the arms of Mr. Benton. 'Get that wretched woman out of my sight. Doctor, is there any chance you can . . .'

The Doctor was already sitting at the computer keyboard. He was flicking almost casually through the thick black book of computer codes. He tossed the book aside. Somehow Sarah knew that every one of those tables had been committed to his amazing memory.

The Doctor pushed back his sleeves, like a virtuoso musician about to give an important recital. His hands started flickering over the keyboard in a blur of speed. As he worked, the Doctor chatted away, his voice light and conversational, as if he was trying to cheer them up. Sarah's eyes kept moving from his intent face to the digital clock. It now read 23, 22, 21 . . .

'The trouble with computers,' said the Doctor chattily, 'is that they're very sophisticated idiots.'

(The clock read 18, 17, 16 . . .)

'They do exactly what you tell them at amazing speed . . .'

(15, 14, 13 . . .)

'. . . even if you order them to destroy you!'

(12, 11, 10 . . .)

'So if you happen to change your mind, it's very difficult to stop them obeying your original order in time . . .'

(6, 5, 4 . . .)

'But not impossible!' concluded the Doctor, sitting back with a final flourish. The digital counter read 3, 2 . . . and stopped there. There was a click and a whirr, and the figures began to whizz upward—until the dial once more stood at a reassuring 600.

Pandemonium broke out in the little control room. The Brigadier, Benton and Harry all crowded round the computer terminal.

'Jolly good show, Doctor,' said the Brigadier.

'Ruddy marvellous,' Harry was shouting. 'Ruddy blooming marvellous!'

From Benton there came only a long, heartfelt, ''Strewth!'

The Doctor got so many hearty slaps on the back that he was in grave danger of being knocked off his chair. His curly hair seemed to stand up round his head with sheer excitement, and the enormous grin on his face was enough to light up the whole room. All Sarah could do was lean weakly against the wall. Now that the crisis was over, she felt tired and drained. She was also shocked by the realisation that she really had been prepared to shoot Miss Winters. What she now wanted more than anything else was a long rest. Suddenly she couldn't bear to stay in the tiny, airless room full of noisy, jubilant men any longer. Unnoticed, she slipped out of the control room. Going along the corridor, she passed the storeroom where she and Harry had been held prisoner. For some reason she stopped and looked inside. It was hard to realise that they had escaped just a little time ago. The two chairs, the strands of broken cord, were exactly as they had left them.

But there was something in the little storeroom that had not been there when Sarah left. A panel in the wall slid open—to reveal the Robot! As Sarah opened her mouth to scream, it reached out and took her neck almost delicately between the fingers and thumb of one great metal hand. So gentle was its touch that Sarah felt only the slightest pressure. She stood quite still and silent, scarcely daring to breathe. The Robot pulled her through the secret panel. It closed behind them, and the storeroom once more stood silent and empty.


Sarah's absence was not at first noticed. There were minor prisoners to be questioned, and reports to be written. The Brigadier and his colleagues were suddenly very busy men.

In fact, the first disappearance to be noticed wasn't Sarah's at all—it was the Robot's. No one could account for its disappearance. When the Brigadier and the others had left the Bunker on their way back to UNIT H.Q., the Robot had been nowhere in sight. The Brigadier had simply assumed that some of his men had carted it away. Similarly, all the UNIT troops had felt sure that someone else had taken charge of it. It wasn't until the Doctor expressed a desire to examine it that its disappearance became apparent. The Brigadier dimly remembered seeing Sarah slipping away from the control room before everyone else, but had assumed that she was going home to rest. It wasn't until he tried contacting her to ask if she'd seen the Robot, that it became apparent that Sarah was also missing.

Irritated by these mysterious events in an affair he'd

thought to be safely concluded, the Brigadier held an enquiry in his office.

The vanishing of Sarah and the Robot was discussed at considerable length. It was the Doctor who first suggested that there might be a connection between the two events.

The Brigadier groaned at the thought of this fresh complication. 'Are you *sure*, Doctor?'

'Oh, I think so, don't you?'

Harry Sullivan scratched his head. 'But why, Doctor? Why should the wretched thing kidnap Sarah?'

The Doctor looked grave. 'It killed Kettlewell, remember, the man who created it. It must be in a traumatic state. It's suffered a tremendous emotional shock!'

The Brigadier was in no mood to waste sympathy on the psychological sufferings of a machine. 'That may be, Doctor, but I still don't see ...'

'Use your intelligence, man. That thing's virtually human. What's more natural than that it should turn to the one person who ever showed it kindness?'

The Brigadier stood up. 'All right, Benton, we go back to Thinktank. Raise every man you can, start at the Bunker, and search outwards from there. Whatever the mental state of our metal friend, I want it found as soon as possible.'

'And Sarah too,' reminded the Doctor. 'Find one and you'll find the other.'

'Yes,' the Brigadier said curtly. 'And Sarah too.'


The room behind the secret panel was surprisingly large and comfortable. Sarah thought it must have been designed as a sort of inner sanctum for VIPs—a place they could retreat to if life in the main Bunker broke down. It was carpeted, well-furnished, and the supplies of food and drink were of a higher standard than in the outer storeroom. She guessed that the Robot must have been hidden there when first taken to the Bunker, and its retentive mind had remembered the hiding place for future use.

Which was all very well, thought Sarah, but it didn't help her to get out of the place alive. The Robot had long ago released its grip on her, and she was free to move about—as long as she didn't go too near the exit panel. She had even managed to make a light meal on tinned lobster and champagne, though under the circumstances her appetite had been far from good. A while ago they had heard the sound of soldiers searching the storeroom, but they hadn't found the secret panel, and Sarah had been far too frightened to call out. Then the sounds had grown fainter, and she had guessed that the search was moving away from them.

She turned to the Robot, speaking with a confidence that she did not feel.

'They're bound to find us in the end, you know.'

'THEY WILL NOT FIND US. EVEN IF THEY DO I SHALL DESTROY THEM'.

'What's the point of that?' said Sarah. 'What's the use of more killing? I keep telling you, it's all over. What can you do on your own?'

'I CAN BRING ABOUT THE DESTRUCTION OF ALL HUMANITY.'

Sarah realised that Kettlewell's prophecy had come true. The mind of the Robot had broken under the strain of all its confusion and suffering. It was completely mad. She flinched away as the great metal hand reached out for her. All it did was touch her very gently upon the shoulder. 'DO NOT FEAR, SARAH. YOU ALONE WILL BE SPARED.'

Once again the Brigadier's Land-Rover was parked in the clump of trees near the Bunker. Harry Sullivan, the Doctor and the Brigadier all stood round it in gloomy silence. They all looked up eagerly as Benton approached, walkie-talkie in his hands.

Benton shook his head. 'Still nothing, sir. We're extending the search area, but the bigger it gets, the thinner we're spread.'

'Tell you something we haven't thought of,' said the Doctor suddenly. 'Just what are we going to do with the thing when we do find it? I mean, I'll try reasoning with it, but I don't promise anything.'

The Brigadier fingered his revolver. 'You know, Doctor, once—just once—it would be nice to meet an alien menace that wasn't immune to bullets.'

Benton coughed. 'Excuse me, sir, but when Professor Kettlewell was at H.Q. chatting—talking—to Miss Smith . . . well . . . he was in a very chatty mood, sir, sort of rambling on.'

'He's not the only one,' snapped the Brigadier. 'Do get to the point!'

'Well, he said something about the Robot being made of a new alloy he'd invented. Called it living metal. I think he even said it could grow.'

The Brigadier gave him a disgusted look. 'Well, that's all very interesting, Mr. Benton. However—'

Desperately Benton floundered on. 'He also said something about a virus, sir. Something that attacked his living metal.'

The Doctor suddenly became interested. 'Did he now? Well, I suppose it's logical enough.'

'So I just thought, sir,' Benton went on, 'if this virus does attack the metal the Robot's made of, maybe we could . . .' His voice tailed off as he realised that the Doctor was staring at him with unnerving intentness. 'Sorry,' he said. 'It's probably a pretty daft idea.'

The Doctor cried, 'Not a bit of it, Mr. Benton. It's a perfectly splendid idea. Brigadier, some transport please. I must get to Kettlewell's laboratory at once.'

The Brigadier waved towards his Land-Rover. 'Take it by all means, Doctor,' he said. 'Mr. Benton, come with me.' He strode away to urge the searchers to new efforts.

The Doctor slid quickly behind the wheel and started the Land-Rover. Harry Sullivan jumped into the back seat, deciding he might as well go with the Doctor as sit about watching the search. A few minutes later, holding on for dear life, he was wondering if he'd made the right decision . . .

The Doctor glanced over his shoulder. 'Nice turn of speed, these things,' he yelled, as they swung on to the main road on two wheels.

Harry nodded and concentrated on staying in the Land-Rover.


In the secret room, the Robot seemed to reach a sudden decision. It pressed the button that opened the hidden panel, and motioned Sarah to go through. They came out into the storeroom. Sarah looked up at the Robot. 'Where to now?'

'WE SHALL RETURN TO THE CONTROL ROOM.'

The Robot led the way along the concrete corridors. The Bunker was deserted now. All prisoners and wounded had long ago been removed. Most of the UNIT troops were being used in the search. One sentry alone had been left to guard the Bunker. Sarah and the Robot turned a corner and almost walked into him. The sentry backed away in horror, raising his gun. The Robot lifted its arm to strike him down. 'No!' Sarah called. 'Don't harm him!' The Robot paused, arm still raised for the blow. Sarah spoke to the sentry in a low, urgent voice. 'Listen, don't shoot. Just leave quietly. Now!'

The sentry opened his mouth to protest. Before he could speak, Sarah continued, 'Please, do as I say. Don't argue and don't try and rescue me. Just go!' To her relief the soldier nodded, sidled cautiously past the Robot, and then ran down the corridor. The Robot lowered its arm and moved on towards the control room as if nothing had happened.

The sentry ran along the corridors towards the main door, which had been left standing open. As he ran towards it he heard a low throbbing. To his horror, he realised that the doors were starting to close. Terrified at the thought of being locked in with the Robot, he burst into a final desperate sprint, and hurled himself through the closing gap just in time, collapsing on the ground as the doors closed behind him. Picking himself up, he headed towards the cluster of UNIT vehicles in a stumbling run...

The Robot moved away from the door control and crossed to the computer terminal. With curious delicacy, its big fingers tapped lightly at the keyboard. The digital clock started to click out the countdown. 600, 599, 598 ...

Suddenly Sarah realised what the Robot was trying to do. 'No!' she sobbed. 'No, you mustn't!' She made a ridiculous attempt to pull it away from the keyboard. A casual flick of the Robot's arm sent her flying across the room. She thudded against a wall, and slid down to the floor. 'Why?' she sobbed. 'Why?'

The Robot spoke without turning. 'I DESTROYED KETTLEWELL. NOW I MUST SEE THAT HIS PLAN DOES NOT FAIL.'

'But Kettlewell changed his mind. He wouldn't *want* you to go on.'

Slowly the Robot swung round to face her. Lights were flashing agitatedly on its forehead, and Sarah could have sworn she could see the anguish in its great metal face. Completely ignoring her arguments about Kettlewell, the Robot replied with a strangely human illogicality. 'ONCE MANKIND IS DESTROYED I SHALL BUILD MORE MACHINES LIKE MYSELF. MACHINES DO NOT LIE. MANKIND IS NOT WORTHY TO SURVIVE.'

The countdown clock ticked remorselessly away.


No one had touched Professor Kettlewell's laboratory since the Doctor's struggle with the Robot. It was still in as much of a shambles as when he left it. After a lengthy search through Kettlewell's chaotic filing system the Doctor finally located some scrawled notes relating to the 'metal virus.' He was now trying to produce the virus itself, watched by a baffled Harry.

Peering at a tattered tea-stained scrap of paper, the Doctor muttered furiously, 'Why didn't the silly man write up his experiments properly? Eh?' He glared at Harry as if it was *his* fault.

The UNIT walkie-talkie on the bench beside the Doctor suddenly crackled into life. 'Doctor, are you there? This is the Brigadier. Do you read me? Over.'

Immersed in his experiments, the Doctor absently swept the squawking radio off the bench. Harry fielded it neatly, flicked the switch and said, 'This is Sullivan, sir. The Doctor's a little preoccupied at the moment.'

'Tell him we've found the Robot!'

Harry said, 'They've found the Robot, Doctor!'

The Doctor poured the contents of one beaker into another and grunted.

Feeling that a warmer response was called for, Harry said, 'Well done, sir. Where is it?'

'In the Bunker. It's locked itself in there with Sarah.'

The Doctor jumped so quickly he almost sent his experiment flying. He began to stride round the laboratory, kicking debris out of his way and talking to himself. 'Now why would it do that? Yes, yes, of course. Oedipal conflict leading to excessive guilt and over-compensation.' He grabbed the walkie-talkie from Harry and snapped, 'Brigadier, the Robot will try to carry out Kettlewell's plan. Is the computer terminal in the bunker still active?'

'I imagine so. No one thought to shut it down.'

'What about the fail-safe procedures—are they still in operation?'

'Far as I know, Doctor. They were set in motion when we first attacked the bunker.'

'Listen to me, Brigadier. Warn all the powers concerned. Fail-safe procedures must not be terminated. They must be continued and speeded up. The emergency is not over.' Tossing the receiver back to Harry, the Doctor returned to his experiment. The fail-safe would work or it wouldn't. In any event he had to continue with his experiment.

Sarah looked on in despair as the countdown ticked into its final phase. Her chief emotion was one of bitter disappointment. To fail like this after all their previous efforts!

The countdown had dropped to double figures by now. 19, 18, 17 . . . Suddenly a light flashed above the keyboard. The ticking of the figures seemed to slow down. An illuminated sign flashed above the terminal. 'CANCEL, CANCEL, CANCEL. FAIL-SAFE PROCEDURE NOW OPERATIVE.' The clock read, 11, 10, 9 . . . and then it stopped. Once again it clicked and whirred its way back to 600. The fail-safe procedures, too late to be of help in foiling Miss Winters, had at least worked in time to prevent this second attempt.

Sarah gasped with relief. 'They used the fail-safe. Please won't you give it up now?'

The Robot stood as if brooding. There was a note of obsession in its voice. 'HUMANITY IS CORRUPT. EVIL. IT MUST BE DESTROYED.'

'How can you take on the whole world? All that will happen is that they'll destroy *you*.'

'DO NOT FEAR. I CANNOT BE DESTROYED. I AM INVINCIBLE.' It touched the control that opened the main doors, and strode from the room. Struggling to her feet, Sarah stumbled after it.

The Brigadier and his men watched as the Bunker doors began to open. The Robot stalked out, Sarah following close behind. The soldiers instinctively raised their weapons as the Robot came nearer.

The Brigadier shouted, 'No one open fire till I give the order. We must give Miss Smith every chance to get clear.' Much good it will do when we *do* fire, he thought. The best they could hope for was a safe retreat, taking Sarah with them. And where was the Doctor when he was needed? Mucking about with chemicals in Kettlewell's laboratory!

The huge metal figure continued its advance. The Brigadier watched it in helpless rage. The enemy was in his sights and he still had no weapon capable of dealing with it. Or had he? Struck by a sudden inspiration, the Brigadier said, 'Mr. Benton, what happened to the Disintegrator Gun after the Robot dropped it? Did we lose that as well?'

Benton shook his head. 'No, sir. Locked it away in the arms truck myself.'

'Then get it—right away!'

Benton ran off and was back in seconds clutching the strange-looking weapon. The Brigadier took it from him. Weird looking thing—but a gun was a gun. . . Cocking mechanism here . . . and a trigger here . . . Grasping it firmly, the Birgadier marched steadily towards the Robot.

As soon as he was within range, he called out to Sarah, 'Miss Smith, run! Get away from it!'

Sarah dashed from the Robot's side and started sprinting for the trees. The Brigadier raised the Disintegrator Gun and fired.

He felt the weapon hum with power in his hands. The Robot glowed fiery red. The Brigadier waited for it to disappear. But it didn't. It *grew* instead. He staggered back in amazement as the Robot grew larger and larger, swelling to the size of a giant.

Looming far above the trees and the buildings the metal colossus strode towards him . . .

12

# The Giant Terror

It was Sarah who saved the astonished Brigadier from being squashed like an ant. She was still running frantically for the trees, aware that something was happening behind her, but not sure what. From its tremendous height, the Robot spotted her scurrying figure. Changing direction, it moved away from the Brigadier and went after Sarah, catching up with her in a few enormous strides.

Sarah screamed as a vast shadow loomed over her, and an enormous metal hand came down from the skies. It scooped her up as a small boy might snatch up a runaway pet mouse. It lifted her up, up, up, until she was on a level with the giant face. This time the booming voice seemed to fill the sky, echoing round the horizon. 'YOU CANNOT ESCAPE. SEE HOW I DEAL WITH OUR ENEMIES.'

The hand stretched out and deposited Sarah carefully on the highest point of the Bunker's tower. She screamed and frantically clutched a concrete ledge, scrabbling for a hold. The Robot turned and strode towards the soldiers.

The Brigadier had to fight to keep his voice steady as the giant Robot marched towards them. 'All of you, into the vehicles,' he ordered. 'Get away from here as fast and as far as you can. I'm staying here to keep it under observation.'

'I'm staying too, sir,' said Benton quietly.

'Then you'd better take cover,' said the Brigadier. Both dived for the nearest ditch.

As the vehicles began to roar away, the Robot was almost upon them. An enormous foot lashed out at the last vehicle to leave, sending the lorry and its crew flying though the air like a discarded toy.

The Brigadier and Benton crouched low. Their only hope lay in not being seen. The UNIT convoy continued its retreat, harried by the Robot like mice by a cat. The giant feet stamped a Land-Rover into twisted metal. It picked up a lorry and flung it across the fields. It landed in a tree, where it hung like some incredible metal bird, the torn canvas of its hood flapping in the wind.

The Brigadier had managed to contact Whitehall on the radio-link, and was pouring out his story to a totally incredulous Cabinet Minister. 'I assure you, sir, I am neither drunk nor mad. The creature exists. Yes, about fifty feet high. It can probably be seen for several miles by now. No, it isn't still growing. We'll need planes, heavy artillery, anything that's available. We may have to use atomic weapons. Look, sir, I've no time to argue with you. Send a spotter plane and call me back. Over and out . . .'

Apparently tiring of its sport with the convoy, the Robot had turned away, allowing the few surviving vehicles to reach the safety of the main road. It stood bestriding the Bunker, as if waiting for fresh opponents to conquer.

Soon a droning sound could be heard high above them. A jet fighter came out of the clouds, wheeled high above the Robot, then disappeared—obviously to report what it had seen. Minutes later, it returned with others. The jet planes began to dive towards the Robot, their rocket cannons streaking out lines of flame. The Robot staggered a little, and then started swatting them like flies.

As the Robot was flailing savagely at the planes, the Doctor and Harry arrived in the Brigadier's Land-Rover. Cautiously, Benton and the Brigadier emerged from hiding. The Doctor nodded towards the angry Robot. 'I see our little problem has grown, Brigadier. What happened?'

The Brigadier looked shamefaced. 'I tried to dispose of it with the Disintegrator Gun.'

'Thereby giving it exactly the colossal infusion of energy it needed to grow. Really, Brigadier!'

Their ammunition exhausted, the jet fighters zoomed away over the horizon. The last of the squadron pulled out of its dive too late, and the giant metal fist smashed it flaming to the ground.

The Brigadier looked away. 'RAF boys didn't have much luck. They'll probably try bombers next time.'

'I very much hope that won't be necessary.' The Doctor nodded towards Harry Sullivan, who was clutching an enormous plastic bucket in which a strange looking fluid sloshed and foamed.

'What the blazes is that stuff, Doctor?'

'Another piece of brilliance from the late Professor Kettlewell. It's an active solution of his "metal virus". With any luck it'll solve all our problems. Hand it over, Harry.'

Harry passed the Doctor the plastic bucket. 'I'll drive you, Doctor.'

'Thank you my boy.' The two men changed places, and Harry started the Land-Rover's engine.

'Now just a minute,' protested the Brigadier. 'Do you really think you can tackle that monster with a bucket of jollop?'

But he was too late. The Land-Rover was already on its way.

It took all Harry's nerve to send the Land-Rover rocketing straight towards the metal monster. He could almost feel one of those huge metal feet coming down to squash them like a bug. They bounced up and down over the torn-up ground, and Harry clung grimly to the wheel. They came closer and closer to the towering metal figure. From the corner of his eye Harry glimpsed a metal hand reaching down to grab them. He swerved frantically, and shot the Land-Rover straight between the Robot's legs. As he did so, the Doctor stood up in his seat and dashed the foaming contents of the bucket over one vast metal foot.

Harry swung the Land-Rover around in a sweeping curve, and headed back to the Brigadier. As they drew up he turned to look at the result of their efforts. At first it seemed they had achieved nothing at all.

The Brigadier said, 'Maybe the stuff won't work now the thing's that size.'

The Doctor shook his head. 'Not a bit of it. It ought to work even faster if anything.' Worriedly he shaded his eyes with his hand and peered at the Robot. It was standing like a colossal statue, the rays of the sun reflected from its huge metallic frame. Suddenly the Doctor gripped the Brigadier's arm. 'Look—the left foot, where I threw the solution . . .'

A rusty brown stain was spreading over the Robot's foot. With amazing speed it began to spread—creeping up the legs, across the body, and along the arms. As the stain spread, the Robot began to shrink smaller, smaller, smaller, until it was back to its normal size. When the transformation was complete, it pitched forward on to the ground and lay motionless.

The Doctor nodded, satisfied. 'Very interesting, that,' he said. 'It threw the growth process into reverse, you see . . .' He began to walk towards the prone figure of the Robot. Harry, Benton and the Brigadier followed him. As they approached, they heard a high-pitched voice coming from somewhere above their heads. 'Help! Help! Please won't someone get me down from here!' They looked up. Sarah, still clinging to the tower of the Bunker, was calling and waving frantically. 'Good grief,' said the Brigadier contritely, 'forgotten all about the poor girl. Mr. Benton, do something about Miss Smith, would you?'

As Benton ran off on his errand of rescue, the three men stood looking down at the Robot. A look of regret appeared in the Doctor's face, but the Brigadier's held only grim satisfaction. 'I'll have it taken away and broken up this time—just in case.'

The Doctor said, 'I don't think there'll be any need for that.' He reached out and touched the Robot with the toe of one shoe. Before their eyes, it crumbled away in to a sort of rusty brown dust. A gust of wind sent it swirling across the ground, and soon there was nothing left. A little sadly, the Doctor turned and walked away.

The Doctor sneaked rather furtively into his own laboratory, scarf round his neck, hat pulled over his eyes. At first, he failed to notice Sarah. She was sitting on a stool gazing sadly into space.

She didn't seem to see the Doctor as he approached. 'Sarah?' he said gently.

She looked up at him, almost on the point of tears. 'Doctor . . . Oh, Doctor . . .'

He sighed. 'I had to do it, you know.'

Sarah gulped, and made a determined effort to control her voice. 'Yes, of course. It was insane at the end, and it had done terrible things. But they made it like that. It's just that, at first, it was so *human*.'

The Doctor put a consoling arm around her shoulders. 'It was a wonderful being, Sarah. Capable of great good, and great evil. Yes, I think you could say it was human.' He fished in his pocket and produced a crumpled paper bag. 'Cheer up,' he said abruptly. 'Have a jelly baby?'

Sarah managed a rather watery smile. She and the Doctor both took jelly babies and munched in silence for a while.

'What *you* need,' said the Doctor, rather indistinctly, 'is a change. How about a little trip in the TARDIS?' He lowered his voice confidentially. 'As a matter of fact, I'm just off myself!'

'Doctor, you can't just *go*!'

'Why can't I? It's a free cosmos!'

'But the Brigadier . . .'

'The Brigadier,' said the Doctor crossly, 'wants me to address the Cabinet, have lunch at Downing Street, dinner at the Palace, and write seventeen reports in triplicate. Well, I won't, I won't, I won't!' The Doctor slammed his fist down on the bench, yelped, and sucked his knuckles.

Reprovingly Sarah said, 'Doctor, you're being childish.'

He looked at her in surprise. 'Of course I am. No point in being grown-up if you can't be childish.' He produced his key and opened the TARDIS door. 'Come with me, Sarah?'

Sarah looked at him. The very idea was ridiculous, of course. She had deadlines to meet, commitments to honour. If she went off in the TARDIS there was no telling where or *when* she'd end up. *Or* what kind of terrifying danger she'd run in to.

She looked at the Doctor. His whole face was alight with mischief and the joy of living. 'Come with me?' he said once more.

Sarah smiled. 'All right,' she said. The Doctor beamed.

As Sarah was about to enter the TARDIS, Harry Sullivan bustled into the lab. 'The Brigadier's after you, Doctor—' He noticed the open TARDIS door. 'Hullo, hullo, and what are we up to now?'

The Doctor had become very fond of Harry, but he was in no mood for interruption. 'Just a little trip,' he said airily.

Harry laughed heartily. 'In that old police box, I suppose?'

'That's right. In that old police box.'

Harry gave a patronising sigh. The Doctor was such a brilliant chap in so many ways. What a pity he still clung to this odd delusion. With the best possible intentions, Harry tried to straighten him out. 'Now then, Doctor, you're a reasonable man, and I'm a reasonable man. And we know police boxes don't go careering about in time and space.'

The Doctor stared at him. 'Do we?'

'Of course we do!'

The Doctor moved a little closer, and lowered his voice. 'Tell you what, old chap, you wouldn't care to step inside for a moment? Just to convince me that it's all an illusion?'

Harry shrugged. 'Well naturally, Doctor, if you think it would help you at all ...'

'Oh it would,' said the Doctor earnestly. 'It would make me feel much better!'

'Now Doctor,' said Sarah warningly. She could well remember the shock of her own first look inside the TARDIS.

The Doctor gave her a wicked grin. He motioned Harry towards the TARDIS. 'In you go, old chap . . .'

And in Harry went. Instead of the little box he had been expecting, he found himself in a huge well-lit control room. A many-sided column filled the entire centre of the room. Obviously he must have gone through some kind of trick door, since the place was bigger on the inside than on the outside; which of course was totally absurd!

The Doctor strode happily across to the console and started manipulating the controls. The door closed behind them. The central section of the console started to rise and fall, and a strange groaning noise filled the air.

Harry turned to Sarah, who stood smiling by his side. 'I say, look here!' he protested.

Sarah patted him on the shoulder. 'Harry, old chap, I'm afraid you're in for a bit of a shock ...'

At the sound of the all-too-familiar groaning noise, the Brigadier came charging down the corridor and into the laboratory. 'Doctor,' he said severely, 'I absolutely forbid you ...'

But he was already too late. The TARDIS faded away before his eyes.

The Brigadier sank down upon a stool. 'Well bless my soul,' he said indignantly. 'He's off again!'

And so he was.

## DOCTOR WHO

| | | | |
|---|---|---|---|
| Δ | 0426116747 | Doctor Who and The Brain of Morbius | 75p |
| Δ | 0426110250 | Doctor Who and The Carnival of Monsters | 85p |
| Δ | 042611471X | MALCOLM HULKE<br>Doctor Who and The Cave-Monsters | 75p |
| Δ | 0426117034 | TERRANCE DICKS<br>Doctor Who and The Claws of Axos | 75p |
| Δ | 042620123X | DAVID FISHER<br>Doctor Who and the Creature from the Pit | 90p |
| Δ | 0426113160 | DAVID WHITAKER<br>Doctor Who and The Crusaders | 75p |
| | 0426114639 | GERRY DAVIS<br>Doctor Who and The Cybermen | 85p |
| Δ | 0426113322 | TERRANCE DICKS<br>Doctor Who and The Daemons | 75p |
| Δ | 042611244X | Doctor Who and The Dalek Invasion of Earth | 85p |
| Δ | 0426103807 | Doctor Who and the Day of the Daleks | 85p |
| Δ | 0426119657 | TERRANCE DICKS<br>Doctor Who and the Deadly Assassin | 85p |
| Δ | 042620042X | Doctor Who—Death to the Daleks | 75p |
| Δ | 0426200969 | Doctor Who and the Destiny of the Daleks | 75p |
| Δ | 0426108744 | MALCOLM HULKE<br>Doctor Who and the Dinosaur Invasion | 75p |

## 'DOCTOR WHO'

| | | | |
|---|---|---|---|
| Δ | 0426103726 | Doctor Who and the **Doomsday Weapon** | **85p** |
| Δ | 0426200063 | TERRANCE DICKS<br>Doctor Who and the **Face of Evil** | **85p** |
| Δ | 0426112601 | Doctor Who and the **Genesis of The Daleks** | **75p** |
| Δ | 0426112792 | Doctor Who and the **Giant Robot** | **85p** |
| Δ | 0426115430 | MALCOLM HULKE<br>Doctor Who and the **Green Death** | **75p** |
| Δ | 0426200330 | TERRANCE DICKS<br>Doctor Who and the **Hand of Fear** | **75p** |
| Δ | 0426201310 | Doctor Who and the **Horns of Nimon** | **85p** |
| Δ | 0426108663 | BRIAN HAYLES<br>Doctor Who and the **Ice Warriors** | **85p** |
| Δ | 0426200772 | TERRANCE DICKS<br>Doctor Who and the **Image of The Fendahl** | **75p** |
| Δ | 0426200772 | Doctor Who and the **Image of The Fendahl** | **75p** |
| Δ | 0426200934 | Doctor Who and the **Invasion of Time** | **75p** |
| Δ | 0426200543 | Doctor Who and the **Invisible Enemy** | **75p** |
| Δ | 0426201256 | PHILIP HINCHCLIFFE<br>Doctor Who and the **Keys of Marinus** | **85p** |
| Δ | 0426110412 | TERRANCE DICKS<br>Doctor Who and the **Loch Ness Monster** | **85p** |

# DOCTOR WHO

PHILIP HINCHCLIFFE
**Doctor Who and the**
Δ    0426118936    **Masque of Mandragora**    85p

TERRANCE DICKS
**Doctor Who and the**
0426201329    **Monster of Peladon**    85p

**Doctor Who and the**
Δ    0426201302    **Nightmare of Eden**    85p

**Doctor Who and the**
Δ    0426112520    **Planet of the Daleks**    75p

**Dr Who and the Planet of**
Δ    0426106555    **the Spiders**    85p

**Doctor Who and the**
Δ    0426201019    **Power of Kroll**    85p

**Doctor Who and the**
Δ    0426200616    **Robots of Death**    90p

MALCOLM HULKE
**Doctor Who and the Sea**
Δ    042611308X    **Devils**    90p

PHILIP HINCHCLIFFE
**Doctor Who and the**
Δ    0426116585    **Seeds of Doom**    85p

IAN MARTER
**Doctor Who and the**
Δ    0426200497    **Sontaren Experiment**    60p

MALCOLM HULKE
**Doctor Who and the**
Δ    0426110331    **Space War**    85p

TERRANCE DICKS
**Doctor Who and the**
Δ    0426200993    **Stones of Blood**    75p

TERRANCE DICKS
**Doctor Who and the**
Δ    0426119738    **Talons of Weng Chiang**    75p

GERRY DAVIS
**Doctor Who and the Tenth**
Δ    0426110684    **Planet**    85p

Wyndham Books are obtainable from many booksellers and newsagents. If you have any difficulty please send purchase price plus postage on the scale below to:

**Wyndham Cash Sales**
**P.O. Box 11**
**Falmouth**
**Cornwall**
OR
**Star Book Service,**
**G.P.O. Box 29,**
**Douglas,**
**Isle of Man,**
**British Isles.**

While every effort is made to keep prices low, it is sometimes necessary to increase prices at short notice. Wyndham Books reserve the right to show new retail prices on covers which may differ from those advertised in the text or elsewhere.

**Postage and Packing Rate**
UK: 40p for the first book, 18p for the second book and 13p for each additional book ordered to a maximum charge of £1·49p. BFPO and EIRE: 40p for the first book, 18p for the second book, 13p per copy for the next 7 books, thereafter 7p per book. Overseas: 60p for the first book and 18p per copy for each additional book.